The Kidnapping of Chewbacca

Somehow, Han managed to lift his head. He could make out, through the machine's rough ride and the distance, the knot of Espos bearing his friend away, a prisoner.

He clawed at the metal under him, to throw himself off the machine, to go back. Rekkon was on him instantly, pinning his arms, with a strength and intensity that were frightening.

"He's my friend!" Han grimaced, writhing.

"Then *help your friend!*" Rekkon urged. "Face hard fact: you must save yourself to save him— and not throw both lives away!"

The giant, imprisoning strength retreated and Han was left enervated, knowing Rekkon was right. Holding the catwalk railing, he stopped staring at the indistinguishable specks of Chewbacca and the Espos.

"Ahh," he lowered his eyes disconsolately, "Chewie . . ."

HAN SOLO
AT STARS' END

From the Adventures
of Luke Skywalker

by Brian Daley

Based on the characters and
situations created by
George Lucas

A Del Rey Book

BALLANTINE BOOKS • NEW YORK

To Poul Anderson and Gordon R. Dickson,
for their kind words to a new guy

and

Owen Lock: learned editor and friend,
who'll race to Antares for pinks, any time

The author wishes to thank Eleanor and
Diana Berry for timely assistance

I

"IT'S a warship all right."

Instrument panels in the *Millennium Falcon*'s cockpit were alive with trouble lights, warning flashers, and the beeps and hoots of the sensor package. Readout screens were feeding combat-information displays at high speed.

Han Solo, crouched forward in the pilot's seat, coolly flicking his eyes from instrument to screen, hastily assessed his situation. His lean, youthful face creased in a frown of concern. Beyond the cockpit canopy, the surface of the planet Duroon drew steadily nearer. Somewhere below and astern, a heavily armed vessel had detected the *Falcon*'s presence and was now homing in to challenge her. That the warship had, in fact, picked up the *Millennium Falcon* first was a matter of no small worry to Han; the ability to come and go without attracting notice, especially official notice, was vital to a smuggler.

He began relaying fire-control data to the ship's weapons systems. "Charge main batteries, Chewie," he said, not taking his eyes from his part of the console, "and shields-all. We're in prohibited space; can't let 'em take us or identify the ship." Particularly, he added to himself, with the cargo we're hauling.

To his right, Chewbacca the Wookiee made a sound halfway between a grunt and a bark, his furry fingers darting to his controls with sure dexterity, his large, hairy form hunched in the oversized copilot's seat. Wookiee-style, he showed his fierce fighting teeth as he rapidly surrounded the starship with layers of defensive energy. At the same time, he brought the *Fal-*

con's offensive weaponry up to its maximum charge.

Bracing his ship for battle, Han berated himself for ever having taken on this job. He'd known full well it could take him into conflict with the Corporate Sector Authority, in the middle of a steer-clear area.

The Authority ship's approach left Han and Chewbacca just seconds for a clutch decision: abort the mission and head for parts unknown, or try to pull off their delivery anyway. Han surveyed his console, hoping for a clue, or a hit off the Cosmic Deck.

The other ship wasn't gaining. In fact, the *Falcon* was pulling away. Sensors gauged the mass, armaments, and thrust of their pursuer, and Han made his best guess. "Chewie, I don't think that's a ship of the line; looks more like a bulk job, with augmentative weapons. She must've just lifted off when she got wind of us. Hell, don't those guys have anything better to do?" But it figured; the one major Authority installation on Duroon, the only one with a full-dress port layout, was on the far side of the globe, where the dawn line would just be lightening gray sky. Han had planned his landing for a spot as far away from the port as possible, in the middle of the night-side.

"We take her down," he decided. If the *Falcon* could shake her follower, Han and Chewbacca could make their drop and, with the luck of the draw, escape.

The Wookiee gave a grumpy growl, black nostrils flaring, tongue curling. Han glared at him. "You got a better idea? It's a little late to part company, isn't it?" He took the converted freighter into a steep dive, throwing away altitude in return for increased velocity, heading deeper into Duroon's umbra.

The Authority vessel, conversely, slowed even more, climbing through the planet's atmosphere, trading speed for altitude in an attempt to keep the *Millennium Falcon* under sensor surveillance. Han ignored the Authority's broadcast order to halt; telesponders that should have automatically given his starship's identity in response to official inquiry had been disconnected long ago.

"Hold deflector shields at full capacity," he ordered. "I'm taking her down to the deck; we don't want our skins cooked off." The Wookiee complied, to shed thermal energy generated by the *Falcon*'s rapid passage through the atmosphere. The starship's controls trembled as she began to buck the denser air. Han worked to put the planet between himself and the Authority vessel.

This he soon accomplished, as indicators registered increased heat from the friction of the freighter's dive. Between watching sensors and looking through the canopy, Han quickly found his first landmark, a volcanically active crevasse that ran on an east-west axis, like a stupendous, burning scar on the flesh of Duroon. He brought the *Falcon* out of her swoop, her control systems rebelling against the immense strain. He leveled off only meters above the planet's surface.

"Let's see them track us now," he said, self-satisfied. Chewbacca snorted. The meaning of the snort was clear—this was temporary cover only. There was little danger of being detected either optically or by instrument over this seam in Duroon's surface, for the *Falcon* would be lost against a background of ferrous slag, infernal heat, and radioactive discord. But neither could she remain there for long.

In the vivid orange light of the fissure that illuminated the cockpit, Han conceded that fact. At best, he'd broken trail so the Authority ship would be unable to spot the *Falcon* should the pursuer gain enough altitude to bring her back into sensor range. He poured on as much airspeed as he dared in an effort to keep Duroon's mass between himself and the vessel hunting him while he sought his landing site. He cursed the fact that there were no proper navigational beacons; this was seat-of-the-pants flying, and no chance of leaning out the cockpit and stopping a passerby for directions.

In minutes the ship had neared the western end of the fissure. Han was compelled to dump some velocity; it was time to look for road signs. He reviewed the instructions given him, instructions he'd committed

3

to memory alone. Off to the south a gigantic mountain range loomed. He banked the *Falcon* sharply to port, slapped a pair of switches, and bore straight for the mountains.

The ship's special Terrain Following Sensors came on. Han kept the freighter's bow close above a surface of cooled lava and occasional active rifts, minor offspring of the great fissure. For whatever small edge it might give against detection, he trimmed the *Falcon* off at virtual landing altitude, screaming over eddied volcanic flatlands. "Anybody down there better duck," he advised, keeping one eye pinned to the Terrain Following Sensors. They bleeped, having located the mountain pass for which he'd been searching. He adjusted course.

Funny. His information said the break in the mountains was plenty wide for the *Falcon,* but it looked mighty narrow on the TFS. For a second he debated going for altitude fast, hurdling the high peaks, but that just might put him back onto the Authority's scopes. He was too close to his delivery point, and a payday, to risk having to cut and run. The moment of option passed. He shed more airspeed, committed now to taking the pass at low level.

Sweat collected on his forehead and dampened his shirt and vest. Chewbacca uttered his low rumble of utmost concentration as both partners synched to the running of the *Millennium Falcon.* The image of the pass on the TFS grew no more encouraging.

Han tightened his grip on the controls, feeling the press of his flying gloves against them. "Pass, nothing —that thing's a *slot!* Hold your breath, Chewie; we'll have to skin through."

He threw himself into a grim battle with his ship. Chewbacca caterwauled his dislike for all unconventional maneuvers as he cut in braking thrusters, but even those would not be enough to avert disaster. The slot began to take on shape, a slightly lighter area of sky lit by bright stars and one of Duroon's three moons, set off by the silhouette of the mountains. It was, just barely, too narrow.

4

The starship took some altitude, and her speed slackened. Those extra seconds gave Han time to pilot for his life, calling on razor-edge reflexes and instinctive skills that had seen him through scrapes all across the galaxy. He killed all shields, since they'd have struck rock and overloaded, and wrenched his controls, standing the *Millennium Falcon* on her portside. Sheer crags closed in on either side, so that the roar of the freighter's engines rebounded from the cliffs. He made minute corrections, staring at rock walls that seemed to be coming at him through the canopy, and rattled off a string of expletives having nothing whatsoever to do with piloting.

There was a slight jar, and the shriek of metal torn away as easily as paper. The long-range sensors winked out; the dish had been ripped off the upper hull by a protrusion of rock. Then the needle's eye was threaded sideways, and the *Falcon* was through the mountains.

Perspiration beading his face, dampening his light brown hair, Han pounded Chewbacca. "What'd I tell you? Inspiration's my specialty!"

The starship soared over the thick jungle that began beyond the mountains. Han leveled off, wiping a gloved hand across his brow. Chewbacca emitted a sustained growl. "I agree," Han replied soberly in the wake of his elation. "That *was* a stupid place to put a mountain." He took up scanning for the next landmark and spied it almost at once: a winding river. The *Falcon* skimmed in low over the watery coils as the Wookiee lowered the ship's landing gear.

In seconds they'd reached the landing area near a spectacular waterfall that dropped two hundred meters to the river in a flume like a blue-white, ghostly scrim under stars and moonlight. Han, reading the TFS, found a clearing in the heavy cover of vegetation and settled the ship slowly. The broad disks of the landing gear sank a bit in soft humus; then the hydrolics sighed briefly as the *Millennium Falcon* made herself comfortable.

Han and Chewbacca sat at their controls for a moment, too drained to do more. Outside the cockpit canopy, the jungle was an irregular darkness, tangles of indefatigable growth topped by a roof of fernlike plants that stretched up twenty meters and more. Gauzy ground fog rolled through the undergrowth and clearing.

The Wookiee gave a long, gusty, bass-register exhalation. "I couldn't have said it better," Han concurred. "Let's get at it." Both removed headsets and left their seats. Chewbacca picked up his crossbow weapon and a bandolier of metal ammo containers, which also supported a floppy carryall pouch at his hip. Han already wore his side arm, a custom-model blaster with rear-fitted macroscope, its front sight blade filed off to facilitate the speed draw. His holster was worn low, tied down at the thigh, cut so that it exposed the weapon's trigger and trigger guard.

According to directories, Duroon's atmosphere would support humanoid life without respirators. The two smugglers moved directly to the ship's ramp. The hatch rolled up and the ramp lowered silently, letting in smells of plant growth, of rotting vegetation, of hot, humid night and animal danger. The jungle was filled with sounds, calls, clacks, and cries of prey and predator, and, over all, with the monumental spillage of the waterfall.

"Now it's up to them to find us," Han said. Checking the jungle, he saw no sign of life. Not surprising. The freighter's landing had probably frightened most wildlife out of the area. He turned to his shaggy first mate/copilot/partner. "I'll wait for them. Turn off sensors, shut down the engines, the works; kill all systems so the Authority can't spot us. Then see how much structural damage she suffered topside when she got her back scratched."

Chewbacca barked acknowledgment and shambled off. Han stripped off his flying gloves, tucked them in his belt, and stepped down the ramp, which stretched down and out from the ship's starboard side, astern the cockpit. He thumbed his gun's sights to set it for night shooting, then glanced around. A lean young

6

man dressed in spaceman's high boots, dark uniform trousers with red piping, and civilian shirt and vest, Han had cast aside his uniform tunic, stripped of its rank and insignia, years ago.

He ran a quick check of the *Falcon*'s underside, assuring himself that she had taken no damage there and that the landing gear had come to rest properly. He also made certain that the interrupter-templates had automatically slid into place along the servoguides for the belly turret, so that the quad-mounted guns wouldn't accidentally blow away the landing gear or ramp if he had to fire them while the ship was grounded.

Satisfied, he went back to the foot of the ramp. He gazed up at the empty sky and the stars beyond, thinking: *Let the Authority look for me; this whole part of Duroon's spotted with hot springs, thermal vents, heavy-metal magma seepages, and radiation anomalies. It'd take them a month to find me, and in an hour or three, I'll be gone like a cool breeze.*

He sat at the end of the ramp, wishing for a moment that he'd brought along something to drink; there was a flask of ancient, vacuum-distilled jet juice under the cockpit console. But he didn't feel like going for it. Besides, he still had business to conduct.

Duroon's nocturnal life forms began reappearing in the mossy clearing. Lacy white things swam through the air with ripples of their thin bodies, resembling flying doilies, while nearby fern-trees held creatures that looked like bundles of straw, making their slow way along the wide fronds. Han kept an eye on them but doubted they'd approach the alien mass of his starship.

As he watched, a smallish green sphere sailed out of the undergrowth in a high arc, landing with a *boink*. It appeared perfectly smooth at first, but then extruded an eyelike bump that studied the *Falcon* with jerky motions. But when it noticed the pilot, it flinched. The eye-bump disappeared, and the spherething's underside compressed. With another *boink* the thing bounced away into the jungle.

Han returned to his musing as he listened to Chewbacca tramping around on the ship's upper hull. The unfamiliar constellations here were how many light-years from the planet of Han's birth? He couldn't even make a close guess.

Being a smuggler and a flyer-for-hire had its dangers, and those he accepted with a philosophical shrug. But a run into a prohibited sector with a cargo that would earn him a summary execution if caught, those were different table stakes altogether.

The Corporate Sector was one wisp off one branch at the end of one arm of the galaxy, but that wisp contained tens of thousands of star systems, and not one native, intelligent species was to be found anywhere. No one was sure why. Han had heard that neutrino research showed abnormalities in the solar convective layers of every sun hereabout, something that might have spread like a virus among the stars in this isolated sector.

In any case, the Corporate Sector Authority had been chartered to exploit—some called it plunder—the uncountable riches here. The Authority was owner, employer, landlord, government, and military. Its wealth and influence eclipsed that of all but the richest Imperial Regions, and the Authority spent much of its time and energy insulating itself from outside interference. Competition, it had none; but that didn't make the Corporate Sector Authority any less jealous or vindictive. Any outside ship found off established trade corridors was fair game for the Authority's warships, which were manned by its feared Security Police.

But what do you do, Han asked himself, when your back's to the wall? How could he have said no to a nice, lucrative run when usurious Ploovo Two-For-One described the riches that were to be had.

I could always hit the beach, he thought. Find a nice planet somewhere, go native. It's a big galaxy.

But he shook his head. No use fooling himself. If he were grounded, he might as well be dead. What could one planet, any planet, offer someone who had knocked around among the stars? The need for the boundless provinces of space was now a part of him.

And so when, broke and in debt, he and Chewbacca had been approached for a run deep into Authority steer-clear territory, they'd jumped at the job. In spite of all the perils and uncertainties, the run still let them raise ship again and experience the freedom of star-travel. Risk of death or capture had been, in their eyes, the lesser of two evils.

But that brought up another point. The Authority ship had somehow picked up the *Millennium Falcon* before her own sensors had detected the other. No doubt the Security Police had something new in the way of detection equipment, thereby making Han's and Chewbacca's lives more complicated by an order of ten. This situation would require immediate future attention.

Han kept a close watch on the jungle around him, wishing he could have left the ship's floodlights on. So, when a voice at his side announced, "We are here," he twisted around with a yelp, his blaster appearing in his fist as if conjured there.

A creature, barely out of arm's reach, was calmly standing next to the ramp. It was almost Han's height, a biped, with a downy, globular torso and short arms and legs boasting more joints than a human's. Its head was small, but equipped with large, unblinking eyes. Its mouth and throat were a loose, pouchy affair; its scent was the scent of the jungle.

"That," Han grumbled, recovering his composure and putting his blaster away, "is a good way to get yourself roasted."

The creature ignored the sarcasm. "You have brought what we need?"

"I've got cargo for you. Beyond that, I know zero, which is the way I want it. If you came alone, you've got your work cut out for you."

The creature turned and made an eerie, piping noise. Figures seemed to grow up out of the ground, dozens of them, motionless, regarding the pilot and his ship with silent gazes. They held short objects of some sort, which he assumed to be weapons.

Then he heard a growl from above. Stepping forward, Han looked up and saw Chewbacca standing out on one of the ship's bow mandibles, covering the newcomers with his bowcaster. Han gave a signal. His hairy first mate put up the bowcaster and headed back inboard.

"Time's wasting," Han told the creature. It moved toward the *Falcon,* taking its companions with it. Han stopped them with upheld hands. "Not the whole choir, friend. Just you, for starters." The first one burbled to its fellows and came on alone.

Inside the ship, Chewbacca had turned up the blackout lights to a minimal glow in strategic parts of the interior. The towering Wookiee was already drawing cover plates off the hidden compartments, concealed and shielded to be undetectable, under the deck near the ramp. Into this space, where he and Han usually hid whatever contraband they were carrying, Chewbacca lowered himself to stand with his waist at deck level. Releasing clamps and strapping, the Wookiee began lifting out heavy oblong cases, the huge muscles beneath his fur bulging with effort.

Han pulled the end of a case around and broke its seals. Within the crate weapons lay stacked. They had been so treated that no part of them reflected any of the scant light. Han took one up, checked its charge, made sure the safety was on, then handed it to the creature.

The firearm was a carbine—short, lightweight, uncomplicated. Like all the others in the shipment, this one was fitted with a simple optical scope, shoulder sling, bipod, and folding bayonet. Though the creature obviously wasn't used to handling an energy weapon, its ready acceptance, grip, and posture showed that it had seen them often enough. It shifted the carbine in its hands, peered down the barrel, and examined the trigger carefully.

"Ten cases, a thousand rifles," Han told it, taking up another carbine. He flipped up its butt plate, pointing out the adapters through which the weapon's power pack could be recharged. These were obsolete weapons by current standards, but they had no internal moving parts and were extremely durable, so much so that they could safely be shipped or stored without Gel-Coat or other preservative. Any one of these carbines, left leaning against a fern in the jungle, would be fully operable ten years from now. Those advantages would be important on this world, where the carbines' new owners would be able to provide little maintenance.

The creature nodded, understanding how the recharging worked. "We have already stolen small generators," it told Han, "from the Authority compounds. We came here because they promised us jobs and a good life, and we celebrated our good fortune, for our world is poor. But they worked us like slaves and would not let us leave. Many of us escaped to live in the wilds; this world is not unlike our own. Now, with these weapons, we will be able to fight back—"

"Stop!" Han snarled with a slashing gesture of his hand, and a violence that made the creature recoil. Reining in his temper, he went on, "I don't want to hear it, get me? I don't know you, you don't know me. It's none of my business, so *don't tell me!*"

The large eyes were fixed on him. He looked away. "I got half my pay on account when I lifted off. The other half comes when I get out of here, so why don't you just take your stuff and scratch gravel? And don't forget: no firing those things until I've left. An Authority ship just might register the noise."

He recalled that advance, paid in glow-pearls, fire nodes, diamonds, nova-crystals, and other precious gems smuggled off this mining planet at terrible risk by whatever sympathizers the contract-slaves had found. Rather than buy their own freedom in a quick dash aboard the *Falcon*, these fugitives were about to throw themselves into a doomed rebellion against the power of the Corporate Sector Authority. Morons.

He stepped out of the creature's way. It watched him for a moment, then went and piped at the open hatch. Others of its kind came scampering up, crowding around the hatch. Their weapons could be seen now, primitive spear-throwers and blowguns. Some carried daggers of volcanic glass. They had clever hands, all three fingers of which were mutually opposable. They filed inboard, surrounding the rifle cases and straining to lift them in teams of sixes and sevens. Chewbacca looked at them in amusement. The cases, being borne away down the ramp and into the jungle, reminded Han of some bizarre funeral procession.

Remembering something, he took the solemn leader aside. "Does the Authority have a warship stationed here? Big-big ship, with lots of guns?"

The creature thought for a moment. "One big ship, which carries cargo, carries passengers. It has big guns on it, and meets other ships up in the sky, to load and unload them, sometimes."

Just as Han had thought. He hadn't encountered a true combat vessel, but rather a heavily armed lighter. Bad, but not as bad as he'd thought. But the creature wasn't finished. "We will need more," it said; "more weapons, more help."

"Consult your clergyman," Han suggested dryly, helping Chewie replace the deckplates. "Or fix up a deal through your own channels, like this run. I'm out; you won't see me again. I'm just doing business."

The creature cocked its head at him, as if trying to understand. Han thrust aside the thought of what life must be like in a forced-labor camp, a driven, joyless existence if ever there was one. That was a common pattern in the Corporate Sector, naive outworlders lured by false promises, signing on only to become prisoners once they reached the compounds. And what could these few fugitives hope to accomplish?

The luck of the draw, he reminded himself. Hits off the Cosmic Deck didn't always make things Right, but Right wouldn't fill an egg timer on Tatooine. You played the cards you got, and Han Solo liked to be on that end of things with the largest profit margin.

But Chewie was staring down at him. Han sighed; the big lug was a good first mate, but a soft touch.

Well, the tip about the Authority ship was worth something—a hint, maybe, a useful lesson. Han snatched the carbine from the leader irritably.

"Just remember this, you're prey. Got me? You've got to think like prey, and use your brains."

The creature understood and moved closer, standing on tiptoe to see what Han was doing with the carbine.

"It's got three settings, see? Safety, single shot, and constant fire. Now, the Security Police here use those riot guns, right? Sawed-off, two-handers? They're real fond of using constant fire, because they can afford to waste power, just hosing it around. You can't. What you do is, lock all your carbines on single shot. And if you get into a firefight at night or in the deep jungle where visibility's poor, shoot at the constant-fire sources. You'll know it's none of your people, so it must be Security Police. You've got to start using your brain."

The creature looked from the man to the carbine and back again. "Yes," it assured him, retrieving the weapon, "we will remember. Thank you."

Han sniffed, knowing how much they still had to learn. And they'd have to learn it on their own, or the Authority would grind them under its vast heel. And on how many worlds, he asked himself, was the Authority doing just that?

His thoughts were interrupted by distant sounds of blaster fire off in the jungle. The creature had moved to the hatch, with its carbine leveled at them. "I am sorry," it told them, "but we had to test some of the weapons here, now, to make certain they work."

It lowered the carbine and fled down the ramp, heading for the jungle. So much for world-saving. "I take it all back," Han said to Chewie as they leaned on the open hatch. "They might do all right at that."

Their long-range sensors had been knocked out by the destruction of the *Falcon*'s dish antenna on the approach run. The ship would have to make a blind lift-off, taking her chances on running into trouble.

Han and Chewbacca stood atop the *Falcon* for

nearly an hour, straining to patch the damaged antenna mount. Han didn't begrudge the time; it had been a worthwhile effort and, if nothing else, had given the fugitives time to leave the rendezvous area. Because, sure as stink in a spacesuit, the *Falcon's* lift-off would be plotted and its point of origin thoroughly searched.

They could wait no longer. The first lightening of the sky would bring every flitter, skimmer, and armed gig the local Authority officials could lay hands on, in a tight visual search grid. Chewbacca, sensing Han's mood, made a snarling comment in his own language.

Han lowered his macrobinoculars. "Correct. Let's raise ship."

They adjourned below, buckled in, and ran through a preflight—warming up engines, guns, shields. Han declared, "I'm betting that lighter will be holding low, where his sensors will do him the most good. If we come up any distance away from him, we can outrun him and dive for hyperspace."

Chewbacca yelped. Han poked him in the ribs. "What's eating you? We just have to play this hand out." He realized he was talking to hear himself. He shut up. The *Millennium Falcon* lifted, hovering for just a moment as her landing gear retracted. Then Han tenderly guided her up through the opening in the jungle's leafy ceiling.

"Sorry," he apologized to his ship, knowing what abuse she was about to take. He fired her up, stood her on her tail, and opened main thrusters wide. The starship screeched away into the sky, leaving the river steaming and the jungle smoldering. Duroon fell away quickly, and Han began to think they had the problem licked.

Then the tractor beam hit.

The freighter shook as the powerful, pulling beam fixed on her. High above, the Authority captain had played it smart, knowing he was looking for a faster, more maneuverable foe. Having outwitted the smuggler, he now brought his ship plummeting down the planet's gravity well, picking up enough speed to compensate for any dodge the *Falcon* might try in her steep climb. The tractor pulled the two ships inexorably into alignment.

"Shields-forward, all. Angle 'em, and get set to fire!" Han and Chewbacca were throwing switches, fighting their controls, struggling desperately to free their ship. In moments it became clear their actions were futile.

"Ready to shift all deflectors astern," Han ordered, bringing his helm over. "It'll have to be a staring match, Chewie."

The Wookiee's defiant roars shook the cockpit as his partner swung the freighter onto a new course, straight at the enemy vessel. All the *Falcon*'s defensive power was channeled to redouble her forward shields. The Authority ship was coming at them at a frightening rate; the distance between ships evaporated in seconds. The Authority lighter, making hits at extreme range, jounced the two around their cockpit but did no major damage.

"Hold fire, hold fire," Han chanted under his breath. "We'll train all batteries aft and kick him going away." The controls vibrated and fought in their hands as the *Falcon*'s engines gave every erg of effort. Deflector shields struggled under a salvo of long-range blaster-cannon fire, lances of yellow-green annihilation. The *Falcon* ascended on a column of blue energy as if she lusted for a fiery double death in collision with her antagonist. Rather than fight the tractor beam, she threw herself toward its source. The Authority ship came into visual range and, a moment later, filled the *Falcon*'s canopy.

At the last instant, the warship's captain's nerve gave. The tractor faded as the lighter began a desperate evasion maneuver. With reflexes that were more like precognition, Han threw everything he had into an equally frantic bank. The two ships' shields couldn't have left more than a meter or two between them in that blindingly fast near miss.

Chewbacca was already shifting all shields aft. The *Falcon*'s main batteries, trained astern, hammered at the Authority vessel at close range. Han scored two hits on the lighter, perhaps no more than superficial damage, but a moral victory after a long, bad night. The Authority ship rocked. Chewbacca howled, and Han exulted, "Last licks!"

The lighter plunged downward, unable to halt her steep dive quickly. The freighter bolted out of Duroon's atmospheric envelope, out into the void where she belonged. Far below her, the Authority vessel was just beginning to pull out of her dive, all chance of pursuit lost.

Han fed jump data into the navicomputer as Chewbacca ran damage checks. Nothing irreparable, the Wookiee decided, but everything would have to have a thorough going-over. But Han Solo and Chewbacca the Wookiee had their money, their freedom, and, for a wonder, their lives. And that, Han thought, should be enough for anyone, shouldn't it?

The starship's raving engines carved a line of blue fire across infinity. Han engaged the hyperdrive. Stars seemed to fall away in all directions as the ship outraced sluggard Light. The *Millennium Falcon*'s main drive boomed, and she disappeared as if she'd never been there.

 II

THEY knew they'd be watched, of course, from the moment they docked their battered freighter.

Etti IV was a planet open to general trade, a world where dry winds swept amber, moss-covered plains and shallow, saline seas beneath vermilion skies. It had no remarkable resources in and of itself, but was hospitable to humans and humanoids and occupied a strategic spot on star-routes.

On Etti IV, great wealth had been gathered by lords of the Corporate Sector, and with this wealth had come its universal corollary, a thriving criminal element. Now, Han and Chewbacca made their way down a street of fusion-formed soil, between low buildings of press-bonded minerals and tall ones of permacite and shaped formex. They wove through the spaceport toward the Authority Currency Exchange, with the Wookiee guiding a rented repulsor-lift handtruck. On the handtruck were cases resembling strongboxes, and it was for that reason that the two assumed they'd be watched. The boxes were just the sort of thing to pique the curiosities of assorted criminal types.

But the duo also knew that any watchers would weigh risk against revenue. In the risk column would be Han's gunman's rig and his loose, confident gait, plus Chewbacca's looming presence and ready bowcaster, not to mention the strength and ferocity to twist any attacker's body into new and different shapes.

So they went their way in confidence, knowing that, as targets, they would appeal to neither the good business sense nor the survival instincts of any would-be stickup artist.

The Authority Currency Exchange had no idea it was abetting a transaction involving gunrunning and insurrection. Han and Chewbacca had already managed to unload the gems with which they'd been paid, exchanging them for precious metals and rare crystalline vertexes. In a Corporate Sector encompassing tens of thousands of star systems, the kind of record-keeping that could keep track of every debt and payment was beyond even the most sophisticated data system. So, without a hitch, Han Solo, tramp freighter captain, smuggler, and freelance law-bender, had converted most of his payment into a nice neat Authority Cash Voucher. If he'd had a hat, he'd have tipped it to the chirping disbursements auto-clerk that spat the voucher at him. He tucked the little plastic chit into a vest pocket.

When they'd left the Exchange, the Wookiee let out one of his long, hooting barks. Han answered, "Yeah, yeah, we'll pay Ploovo Two-For-One, but first we've got one stop to make."

His sidekick growled loudly, startling bystanders with his displeasure and inviting a dangerous sort of attention. A detachment of Security Police appeared out of the swirl of humans, 'droids, and nonhumans moving along the street.

"Hey, lighten up, pal!" Han murmured out of the side of his mouth. The brown-uniformed Security Police, their suspicious eyes darting beneath battle helmets, sauntered along four abreast, their weapons held ready, as pedestrians moved quickly out of their way. Han saw two of the black battle helmets bob, and knew they'd heard the Wookiee's outburst. But the disturbance apparently didn't merit their attention, and the detachment went its way.

Han stared after them, shaking his head. There were all kinds of cops in the galaxy, some of them good, some not. But the Authority's private Security Police—"Espos," in slangtalk—were among the worst. Their enforcements had nothing to do with law or justice, but only with the edicts of the Corporate Sector Authority. Han had never been able to figure out what turned a man into an unquestioning Espo bully-boy; he merely tried to insure that he didn't cross trails with any of them.

Remembering Chewbacca, he resumed their conversation. "Like I say, we'll pay Ploovo. This stop-off won't take a minute. We'll meet him right after, like we planned, square things, and go our way free and clear."

The placated Wookiee carped noncommittally but fell in beside his partner again.

Because Etti IV's monied classes required conspicuous means of demonstrating their wealth, the spaceport harbored several exotic pet stores, featuring rare or unique stock from the immeasurable expanses of the Empire. *Sabodor*'s was, by general consensus, the best of them. It was there that Han went.

The store's muting system, expensive as it was, couldn't mask all the scents and sounds of the curious life forms somewhat loosely collected there under the dubious classification: *Pets*. Among the species on display were such premium specimens as the spidery night-gliders of Altarrn, the iridescent-feathered song serpents from the deserts of Proxima Dibal's single planet, and the tiny, tubby, clownish marsupials from Kimanan that were commonly called furballs. Cages and cases, tanks and environmental bubbles, teemed with glowing eyes, restless tentacles, clicking chelae, and wobbling pseudopodia.

The proprietor instantly appeared, Sabodor himself, a denizen of Rakrir. His short, segmented, tubular body scuttled along on five pairs of versatile limbs, his two long eyestalks moving and rotating constantly. Seeing the pair, Sabodor rose up on his last two sets of limbs, his uplifted eyestalks reaching nearly to the level of Han's chest, inspecting him from all angles.

"Ever so sorry," Sabodor's voice twittered from the cantilevered vocal organ located at the center of his midsection. "I don't deal in Wookiees. They're a sentient species; can't use them as pets. Illegal. I've got no use for a Wookiee."

Chewbacca cut loose with a furious roar, showing his fearsome teeth, stamping a hairy foot the size of a platter. Display racks shook and cases vibrated. Emitting a squeal, the terrified Sabodor scooted past Han, his foremost limbs clapped over his hearing orifices. The pilot tried to calm his big friend, while dozens of pets began chorusing their answering chitters, hums, screams, and tweets, bouncing around their respective confinements in fear and agitation.

"Chewy, easy! He didn't mean it," Han soothed, blocking the Wookiee from a violent laying of hands upon the quivering shopkeeper.

Sabodor's trembling eyestalks appeared, one to either side of Han's knees. "Tell the Wookiee no offense.

An honest mistake, was it not? No insult intended."

Chewbacca quieted somewhat. Han, remembering all the Security Police in port, was grateful. "We came in to buy something," he told Sabodor as the proprietor rippled away from him in reverse gear. "Hear me? Buy."

"Buy? Buy! Oh, come, sir, and see-see-see! Any pet worth having is to be had at *Sabodor*'s, best in the Sector. We have—"

Han had waved him to silence. He laid a friendly hand on the spot where the overwrought little shopkeeper's shoulder would have been, if he'd had one. "Sabodor, I'm going to make this transaction easy. What I want is a Dinko. You have one?"

"Dinko?" Sabodor's tiny mouth and olfactory cluster somehow cooperated with his recoiling eyestalks to convey disgust. "What for? A Dinko? Revolting, ugh!"

Han's mouth tugged in a wry smile. He produced a handful of cash, riffling it invitingly. "Got one for me?"

"Can do! Wait right here!" Sabodor, undulating excitedly, flowed away into a back room. Han and Chewbacca barely had time to gaze around before the proprietor was back. In his upper two pairs of appendages he held a clear case. Inside was the Dinko.

Few creatures enjoyed the dubious notoriety accorded to Dinkoes, whose temperament came quite close to pure psychopathy. One of the mysteries of the zoological world was how the little terrors tolerated one another long enough to reproduce. Small enough to fit in a man's palm—if that man were indiscreet enough to pick it up—the Dinko glowered out at them. Its powerful rear legs moved constantly, and the twin pairs of grasping extremities on its chest pinched the air, longing for something upon which to fasten. Its long tongue flickered in and out between wicked, glittery fangs.

"Is it de-scented?" Han asked.

"Oh, no! And it's been in rut ever since it was transshipped. But it's been de-venomed."

Chewbacca grinned, his black nose wrinkling.

Han asked, "How much?"

Sabodor named an exorbitant sum. Han counted through his sheaf of cash. "I'll give you exactly one half that, agreed?"

The eyestalks, flopping about in distress, seemed close to tears. The Wookiee, snorting, leaned down at Sabodor, who shrank again behind the dubious safety of Han's knees. "Admit it, Sabodor," Han invited cheerfully, "it's a good deal."

"You win," wailed the proprietor. He proffered the case. The Dinko threw itself from side to side of its container, foaming at the chops.

"One more thing," Han added blithely. "I want you to give it a light sedation dosage so I can handle it for a moment. Then you can give it to me in a different box, something opaque."

That was really *two* things, but Sabodor agreed dejectedly, eager to have the Wookiee, the human, and the Dinko all out of his establishment as soon as possible.

Ploovo Two-For-One, loan shark and former robber, smash-and-grab man, and bunko-steerer out of the Cron Drift, looked forward with pleasure to collecting the outstanding debt from Han Solo.

He was elated, not only because the original loan would reap a splendid profit for himself and his backers, but also because he thoroughly hated Solo, and an interesting form of revenge had materialized.

The message from Solo, promising repayment, had stipulated a meeting here on Etti IV, in the spaceport's most elegant bistro. That had been all right with Ploovo Two-For-One; his creed was that toil and enjoyment should be combined whenever feasible. *The Free-Flight Dance Dome* was more than satisfactory; it was opulent. Ploovo himself was far from charming, a bad-tempered hulk of a man whose face was subject to a nervous tic; but his income gave him a certain conspicuous social viability.

He sprawled onto a conform-lounger at a corner table, joined by the three retainers he'd brought along. Two of these were humans, hard-bitten men with a number of weapons concealed on and about their persons. The third was a long-snouted, scaly-skinned biped, native of Davnar II, who possessed a true flair for execution.

Ploovo, flashing more than enough currency to create an inspired sense of hospitality in the waitress, primped at his black, oily topknot. While he waited, he gloated over his anticipated revenge on Han Solo. Not that the pilot wouldn't repay. The loan shark was certain of getting his money. But Solo had long been an irritant, always ready with some dazzling evasion of payment, jeering Ploovo and bewildering him at the same time. On a number of occasions Ploovo had lost face with his backers because of run-ins with Solo, and his backers weren't the sort to be amused by that. The code of ethics necessary to the conduct of illegal enterprises kept Ploovo from turning in the captain-owner of the *Millennium Falcon* to the law; nevertheless, a convenient local circumstance would serve the loan shark's purpose just as well.

Entering with Chewbacca beside him, a metal case in hand, Han Solo appraised *The Free-Flight Dance Dome* with a great deal of approval.

As on almost any civilized planet, many species mixed and mingled here in a taxonomic hodgepodge, their appearance familiar or alien by turns. Having seen about as much of the galaxy as a man might reasonably expect to, Han still found he couldn't identify half the nonhuman types he saw here. That wasn't unusual. The stars were so many that no one could catalog all the sentient races they'd spawned. Han had lost count of the times he'd entered a room like this one, filled with a kaleidoscope of strange shapes, sounds, and odors. Without straining, he could spot a dozen types of respirators and life-support apparatus being used by entities whose biology wasn't compatible with standard human atmosphere.

Han particularly appreciated those human and near-human females dressed in shimmersilks, chromasheaths, and illuminescences. One swept up to him, fresh from the bank of coin-games that offered such diversions as Mind-Jam, Senso-Switch, Reflex Races, and Starfight. She was a tall, lithe girl with a wine-dark cast to her skin and hair like plaited silver, wearing a gown that seemed to have been knit from white mist. "Welcome down, spaceman," she laughed, throwing an arm around him. "How about a turn through the dance dome?"

Han shifted his burden to his other arm as Chewbacca looked on disapprovingly; several of their less auspicious adventures had begun just this way. "Sure!" Han responded enthusiastically. "Let's dance, let's snuggle up, let's get *grafted together!*" He gently pushed her away. "A little later."

She showed him a truly stunning smile—to let him know it was nothing personal—and moved on to greet another customer before he'd moved out of earshot.

The Free-Flight Dance Dome was a first-class trough. It was equipped with a top-of-the-line gravity field, its console visible among the bottles, spigots and taps, and other paraphernalia encircled by the bar. The field permitted the management to alter gravity anywhere on the premises, and so the dance floor and the dome over it had become a low-gee acrobatic playground in which singles, couples, and groups looped, floated, and spun with effortless grace. Han also spotted individual booths and tables where species from low-gravity worlds were taking their ease in comfort, the specific gravity of their area having been lowered for them.

Han and Chewbacca moved further into the twilight of the place, hearing the clink of drinking vessels of many kinds and the interweaving of any number of languages over the blast from the sound system. They breathed in the aromas of diverse inhalants and aerosols; a profusion of smoke and vapors of various hues, defying the ventilation unit, had drifted by thermoclines into multicolored strata.

He had no problem spotting Ploovo Two-For-One; the big glom had found a large table in the corner, the better to watch for his debtor. Han and Chewbacca sauntered over. Ploovo applied a labored, unconvincing smile to his well-upholstered face. "Solo, old colleague. Come, sit."

"Spare us the guano, Two-For-One." Han sat down next to Ploovo. Chewbacca slung his bowcaster over his shoulder and took a place across the table so that he and Han could watch each other's backs. Han set down the box he carried. Ploovo's greedy eyes caressed it. "Feel free to drool," Han bade him.

"Now, Solo," Ploovo chided, volubly ready to ignore any insult in the heady presence of money, "that's no way to talk to your old benefactor." Ploovo had already been informed by contacts here that these two freighter bums had exchanged a large quantity of negotiables for cash. His hand went for the box. Han's got there first.

The pilot challenged the loan shark with a raised eyebrow. "Your payment's in there. With interest. We're quits after this, Ploovo."

Strangely unperturbed, Ploovo nodded, his topknot jiggling along with his jowls. Han was about to question this when Chewbacca's warning snarl interrupted. A detail of Security Police had entered *The Free-Flight*. Some stationed themselves at the doors while the others made their way around the room.

Han snapped the retaining strap off his holstered blaster. The sound made Ploovo turn. "Now, um, Solo, I swear I had nothing to do with this. We are, as you so recently pointed out, quits. Even *I* wouldn't presume to turn informer and risk my livelihood." He put a fat, covetous hand on the box. "I believe those gentlemen in institutional brown are seeking a man who answers your description. While I no longer have any interest in your well-being, I suggest that you and your fuzzy comrade absent yourselves from here at once."

Han didn't waste time wondering how the Authority had gotten on his tail after he'd obtained new registration for the *Falcon* and identification certificates for himself and Chewbacca. He leaned close to Ploovo, right hand still close to his blaster.

"Why don't we just sit here awhile, *colleague?* And

24

as long as we're at it," he addressed Ploovo's flunkies, "you all have my permission to put your hands right up on the table here, where Chewie and I can see them. *Now!*"

Ploovo's upper lip beaded with sweat. If anyone made a play now, he would certainly become corpse number one. He stuttered an order; his men complied with Han's proposal.

"Compose yourself, Solo," Ploovo implored, though Han was quite serene; it was Ploovo's face that had become pasty white. "Don't let that, er, renowned temper get the better of you. You and the Wookiee can be so irrational at times. Take the occasion when Big Bunji was careless enough to forget to pay you, and you two strafed his pressure dome. He and his staff barely had time to get into their survival suits. Things like that give a man a bad reputation, Solo!" Ploovo was shaking now, having very nearly forgotten his money.

The Security Police had been circulating. They stopped by the table, two rankers and a sergeant. Their timing couldn't have pleased Ploovo less.

"Everyone at this table, produce identification."

Chewbacca had assumed his most innocent expression, his big, soft blue eyes upturned to the soldiers. He and Han offered their falsified IDs. The pilot's hand hovered near his weapon's grip, even though a shootout now, in this position and at these odds, with the door firmly held by reinforcements, held little promise of survival.

The Espo sergeant ignored the credentials of Ploovo and his gang. Skimming Han's, he asked, "These are correct? You're the master-owner of that freighter that made planetfall today?"

Han saw no margin for deception there. And if the Authority had already connected his new persona with events surrounding the illegal landing on Duroon, he was as good as dead. Still, he managed to look faintly amused and somewhat bewildered by all this interrogation.

"The *Sunfighter Franchise?* Why, yes, Officer. Is

anything wrong?" Guileless as a newborn, he gazed up at them.

"We got your description from the docking bays supervisor," the Security Police sergeant answered. "Your ship's been impounded." He threw the IDs back on the table. "Failure to conform to Authority safety standards."

Han's mental processes switched tracks. "She's got all her approvals," he objected, thinking he ought to know, having forged them himself.

The Espo waved that away. "Those're outdated. Your ship fails to meet new standards. The Authority redefined ships' performance profiles, and from what I heard, buddy, your freighter violates hers about ten different ways and doesn't appear on the Waivers List. Just on external inspection, they found her lift/mass ratio and armaments rating way out of line for nonmilitary craft. It looks like a lot of radiation shielding got removed when the thruster ducting was chopped and rechanneled. Also, she's got all that irregular docking tackle, augmented defensive shields, heavy-duty acceleration compensators, and a mess of long-range detection gear. That's some firecracker you've got there."

Han spread his hands modestly; this was one time when he didn't feel like boasting about his pride and joy.

The Espo sergeant went on. "See, when you run a hot rig like that, small payload, overmuscled, the Corporate Sector Authority starts thinking you might take a notion to do something illegal with it. She'll have to be refitted to original specs; you'll have to appear and make arrangements."

Han laughed airily. "I'm positive there's some error." He knew he'd been lucky they hadn't forced the locks for an inboard search. If they'd seen the anti-sensor equipment, jamming and countermeasures apparatus, and broad-band monitoring outfit, this would have been an arrest party. And what if they had found the contraband compartments?

"I'll drop by the portmaster's office as soon as my

business is done," Han promised. He now realized that this was why Ploovo Two-For-One had been so content. The loan shark hadn't even had to violate criminal protocol or risk his own rank hide going against Han and Chewbacca; Ploovo had known the *Millennium Falcon,* under any name, would run afoul of these Authority regulations.

"No good," the Espo sergeant was saying. "My orders are to escort you down as soon as you're found. The portmaster wants this matter cleared up right away." The Espos were suddenly more alert.

Han's smile became pained and sympathetic. Platitudes of understanding rolled from him. Meanwhile, he considered his dilemma dispassionately. The Authority would want a full accounting of ship's papers, log, master's credentials. When those showed discrepancies, there'd be a full ID scan: pore patterns, retinal and cortical indexes—the whole routine. Eventually, they'd find out who Han and his first mate were, and then the trouble would really start.

It was axiomatic to Han Solo's philosophy that you never go one step closer to jail than necessary. But seated here, he could offer no decent resistance. He shot a glance at Chewbacca, who was amusing himself by showing his teeth to the wary Security Police in a frightening smile. The Wookiee caught Han's look, though, and inclined his head slightly.

Whereupon the pilot rose. "Shall we get this unpleasantness taken care of, then, Sergeant, so we can all go our way?" Chewie shuffled away from the table, his attention on Han, one paw on the sling of his bowcaster. Han leaned down for a last word with Ploovo.

"Thanks for the good time, old colleague. We'll get back to you as soon as we can, I promise. And before I forget, here's your payment." He flipped down the box's front end and stepped back.

Ploovo dug into the box, expecting to fill his itchy palm with wonderful, sensuous money. Instead, sharp little fangs clamped down on the fleshy part of his thumb. Ploovo screamed as the enraged Dinko swarmed out and sank its needlelike claws into his pudding of a stomach. Fastened to the Dinko's dorsal vane was the Authority Cash Voucher, Han's thoughtful way of repaying debts both financial and personal —with interest.

The Espos' attention switched to the table as the criminal boss howled. One of Ploovo's henchmen tried to tear the Dinko off his employer while the others gaped. The Dinko wasn't having any; it slashed the fumbling hands with the serrated spurs on its rear legs, then sprayed everyone at the table with vile squirts from its scent sac. Few things in nature are more repugnant than a Dinko's defensive secretion. Men and humanoid fell back, coughing and gagging, forgetting their boss.

The Security Police were trying to understand what was happening as beings stumbled from the table, lurching past them, leaving Ploovo to the mercies of the rabid little beast. The Dinko was now trying energetically—if overoptimistically—to devour him, starting with his nose, which rather reminded it of one of its many natural enemies.

"*Yahhh!*" Ploovo complained, wrenching at the determined Dinko. "Ged it off of be!"

"Chewie!" was all Han had time to yell. He punched the nearest Espo, not wanting to shoot at close quarters. The Espo, caught off guard, fell backward, thrashing. Chewie did better, picking up the other two by their harnesses and bashing them together helmet to helmet, eliciting a gonging sound from the ultrahard surfaces. Then the Wookiee ducked into the crowd with notable agility, following his friend.

The Espos at the doors were unlimbering wide-bore, shoulder-fired blasters, but the confused crowd was milling around and no one had a clear idea yet of just what was going on. The antigrav dancers began alighting as beings raised their attention from assorted intoxicants, stimulants, depressants, psychotropics, and placebos. The room buzzed with a sort of befuddled, translingual *"Huh?"*

Ploovo Two-For-One, having finally dissuaded the

Dinko from his abused nose by main force, flung it across the room. The Dinko landed upon the dinner of a wealthy dowager, destroying the appetite of everyone at that table.

Ploovo, still caressing his wounded snout, turned just in time to see Han Solo vault the bar. "There he is!" the underworld boss exclaimed. The two bartenders rushed to stop Han, swinging the stun-staves they kept behind their bar for the preservation of order. He met the first with crossed wrists intersecting the bartender's, stopping the descending stun-stave, brought his knee up, and elbowed the first mixologist into the second. Chewbacca, following his partner over the bar with a joyous bellow that made the lighting fixtures tinkle, fell on top of the bartenders.

A blaster bolt, fired by one of the Espos at the doors, shattered a crystalline globe of four-hundred-year-old Novanian grog. The crowd bleated, most of them diving for the floor. Two more shots blew fragments out of the bar and half slagged the cash repository.

Han had struggled past the vigorous tangle of Chewie and the bartenders. He grabbed for his blaster and threw down on the Espos, peppering their general location with short bursts. One dropped, his shoulder smoking, and the others scattered for cover. Off to one side, Han could hear Ploovo and his men clubbing their way through yelling, charging customers. He headed for the bar.

Han turned to his objective, the gravity controls. With no leisure to analyze them, he frantically began moving indicators toward maximum. Luckily for everyone not within the insulated area of the bar, he noticed when he'd happened on the general field override, and there were no longer any free-flight dancers in the air. Thus, no one was crushed, or dashed to smithereens.

As it was, Han ran the place's gee-load up to three-point-five Standard. Entities of all descriptions sank to the carpets, borne down by the staggering weight of their own bodies, proving there were no heavy-gee natives here today. The Espos flopped with the rest. Ploovo Two-For-One, Han noted in passing, strongly resembled a beached bloatfish.

There was silence except for the grunts of determined breathing and the smothered groans from those who'd suffered some minor mishap in hitting the deck. No one seemed badly hurt, though. Han put his smoking blaster away, studying the gravity-field's controls, telling himself, *Yo, now; what we need is a tight corridor out of here.* But he was biting his lip, and his fingers poised indecisively over the adjustments.

With an impatient hoot, Chewbacca, who'd put away both bartenders, picked Han up by the shoulders and set him aside. The Wookiee stood over the console, his long fingers moving with nimble precision, peering frequently from his work to the door. In moments the bodies of the two or three patrons lying along his corridor of lighter gravity stirred weakly. Everyone else, the Espos and Ploovo's underworld contingent included, remained pasted to the floor.

Chewbacca eased himself carefully back over the bar and into the normal-gee passageway. He clamored smugly to Han.

"Well, *I* was the one who thought of it, wasn't I," the pilot groused, trailing after his friend. Outside the Free-Flight, he discreetly closed the doors behind him and straightened his clothes, while Chewie gave himself a fastidious brushing.

"Hey, Chewie, you were slow with your left just now, weren't you?" Han queried. "Is your speed going, old-timer?" Chewbacca belched savagely; age was a standing joke between them.

Han stopped a group of laughing revelers who'd been about to enter the *Free-Flight.* "This establishment is officially closed," he proclaimed with weighty importance. "It's quarantined. Fronk's Fever."

The merrymakers, intimidated by the sinister sound of that imaginary malady, didn't even think to question. They left at once. The two weary partners grabbed the first robo-hack they saw, and sped off toward their ship.

"Things are getting tough for the independent businessman," Han Solo lamented.

 III

SEVERAL minutes later, the robo-hack deposited Han and Chewbacca around the corner from their docking bay, Number 45. They'd decided it would be wise to scout the landscape to determine whether the forces of law, order, and corporate dividends had gotten there first. Peering cautiously around the corner, they saw a lone portmaster's deputy dutifully locking an impoundment-fastener on their bay's blast doors. Han pulled his first mate back into concealment for a conference. "No time to wait until the coast is clear, Chewie; they'll be sorting things out back at the *Free-Flight* any time now. Besides, that geek is about to lock up the bay, and Espo patrols would get kind of curious if they saw us burning our way through the blast doors."

He peeked out again. The deputy had nearly finished making connections between alarms and the blast-door solenoids. No doubt the bay's other door was fastened as well. Han looked around and noticed an Authority liquor and drugs outlet to his rear. He took his partner's elbow.

"Here's the plan . . ."

A minute later, the portmaster's deputy had wrestled the massive lock halves into place and finished securing the impoundment-fastener. The blast doors slid shut with a shrinking of diamond-shaped opening that disappeared with a clang. The deputy pulled a molecularly coded key from its slot in the fastener, and the device was activated. Now if it were disturbed or damaged, it would instantly inform Espo monitors.

The deputy tucked the key into his belt pouch and prepared to report his errand completed. Just then a Wookiee, a big, leering brute, came wandering past in a drunken stagger, with a sloshing ten-liter crock of some vile-smelling brew cradled in his thick, hairy arm. Just as the Wookiee drew even with the deputy, a man coming from the other direction failed to avoid the shambling creature's dipsomaniacal lurches. There was a rapid, complicated three-way collision, resulting in the Wookiee's stumbling into, and spilling his liquor all over, the luckless deputy.

The instant pandemonium included accusation and counteraccusation, all in raised voices. The Wookiee gobbled horribly at both men, shaking knotted fists and gesturing to the spilled crock. The portmaster's deputy was brushing uselessly at his soaked tunic. The other participant in the accident did his best to be of help. "Oh, say, that's really a shame," Han *tsk*ed with a sad, solicitous tone. "Hey, that stuff's really in there, huh," he said as he tried to wring some of the brew out of the tunic fabric. The deputy and the Wookiee were swapping inprecations and contradictory claims about whose fault the accident had been. The occasional passerby kept right on moving, not wishing to become involved.

"Fella, you better get that tunic washed right away," Han advised, "or that smell'll never come out."

The deputy, with a last threat of legal action against the Wookiee, stalked off. His pace quickened as he realized with apprehension that a supervisor might happen by at any time and catch sight—or even worse, a whiff—of him. He hurried on, leaving the other two to argue liabilities and culpabilities.

The argument stopped as soon as the deputy was gone. Han held up the key he'd lifted from the deputy's belt pouch during the confusion. He handed it to Chewbacca. "Go warm up the ship, but don't call for clearance. The portmaster's most likely got us posted for grounding. If there's a patrol ship, it'd be on our necks in no time." He estimated that eight minutes had passed since they'd fled the *Free-Flight;* their luck couldn't hold much longer.

Chewbacca ran a hasty preflight while Han dashed off along the row of docking bays. He passed three before he came to the one he wanted. In it was a stock freighter, not unlike what the *Millennium Falcon* had once been, but this one was clean, freshly painted, and shipshape. Her name and ID symbols were proudly displayed on her bow, and labor 'droids were busily loading general cargo under the supervision of her crew, who looked nauseatingly honest. Han leaned through the open blast doors, waving a friendly hand. "Hi there. You guys still raising ship tomorrow?"

One of them waved back, but looked confused. "Not tomorrow, bud; tonight, twenty-one hundred planetary time."

Han feigned surprise. "Oh? Well, clear skies." The crewman returned the traditional spacer's farewell as Han strolled away casually. As soon as he was out of their sight, he took off at a run.

When he got back to Bay 45, he found Chewbacca finishing locking the impoundment-fastener on the inner sides of the blast doors, reconnecting them. Han nodded approvingly. "Bright lad. Are we revved up?"

The Wookiee yipped an affirmative and slid the blast doors shut. Locking them again, this time from the inside, he threw the molecularly coded key away.

Han had already reached his seat in the cockpit. Taking his headset, he called port control. Using the name and ID code of the freighter down in Docking Bay 41, he requested that liftoff time be moved up from twenty-one hundred planetary time to immediately, not an unusual request for a tramp freighter, whose schedule might change abruptly. Since there wasn't much traffic and clearance for that ship had already been granted, immediate liftoff was approved at once.

Chewbacca was still buckling in when Han raised

ship. Her thrusters flared, and the *Falcon* made, for her, a moderate and restrained departure from Etti IV. When the Espos showed up at Docking Bay 45 and cut their way in, Han reflected, they'd have one interesting time trying to figure out how somebody had sneaked a starship out from under the portmaster's nose.

The starship parted company with Etti IV's gravitational field. Chewbacca, elated over what had been a fairly nifty escape, was in high spirits. The Wookiee's leathery muzzle was peeled back in a nice-hideous smirk, and he was singing—or what passed among his people as singing—at the top of his capacious lungs. The volume of it, in the confides of the cockpit, was incredible.

"C'mon, Chewie," Han implored, rapping a gauge with his knuckle, "you're making all the instruments jump." With a behemothish sort of yodel, the Wookiee ceased. "Besides," Han continued, "we're not out of the heavy weather yet."

Chewbacca lost his placid look and lowed an interrogative. Han shook his head. "Naw, Ploovo's got his money; no matter how torqued off he is, his backers'll never unpocket for a contract on us now. No, what I meant was, the long-range dish we patched together won't last forever. We need another, a top-of-the-line model. Besides, the Espos and, I guess, most other folks who like to arrest people have some kind of new sensor that evades detection on old equipment. We need one of those, too, to get back over with the smart money. One more thing—we need one of those Waivers if we've going to operate around here; we have to wrangle ourselves onto that list somehow. Dammit, the Corporate Sector Authority's wrung out thousands of solar systems; I can almost smell that money! We ain't passing up on fat pickin's just because somebody around here doesn't like our lift/mass ratio."

He finished plotting his hyperdrive jump and turned to his partner with a sly grin. "Now, since the Authority doesn't owe you and me any personal favors, what's that leave?"

The long-pelted first mate growled once. Han spread a hand on his chest and pretended to be shocked. "Outside the law, did you say? *Us?*" He chuckled. "Right you are, pal. We'll take so much money off the Authority we'll need a knuckle-boom to haul it all away."

The hyperdrive began to cut in. "But first, it's time to meet and greet old friends. After that, everybody'd best hang on to their cash with both hands!" Han finished.

They had to do it in steps, of course. A hyperspace jump took them to an all-but-deserted, played-out mining world where the Authority didn't even bother to maintain offices. A lead there, from an old man who had once seen better days, put them in touch with the captain of a long-orbit ore barge. After some finagling, during which their *bona fides* were checked, with their lives forfeit if that check had turned up the wrong answers, they were given a rendezvous.

At that rendezvous they were met, in deep space, by a small ship's gig. When an inboard search by armed, wary men revealed that the *Falcon* carried no one but her pilot and copilot, the two were led to the second planet of a nearby star system. The gig parted company with them, and they came in for a landing, tracked by the upraised snouts of turbo-laser cannons. The site was a huddle of quickly assembled hanger domes and habitation bubbles. Parked here and there was a wide assortment of ships and other equipment, much of it gutted and decaying, cannibalized for spare parts.

When Han stepped down the starship's ramp, his face lit with that intense smile that had been known to make men check up and see what their wives were doing. "Hello, Jessa. It's been too long, doll."

The woman waiting at the foot of the ramp looked back at him scornfully. She was tall, her hair a mass of heavy blond ringlets, and her shape did extremely pleasant things to the tech's coveralls she wore. Her upturned nose held a collection of freckles acquired under a variety of suns; Jessa had been on almost as many planets as Han. Just now, her large brown eyes showed him nothing but derision.

"Too long, Solo? No doubt you've been busy with religious retreats? Mercantile conferences? Mild deliveries for the Interstellar Childrens' Aid Fund? Well, it's no wonder I haven't heard from you. After all, what's a Standard Year, more or less, hey?"

"A lifetime, kid," he answered smoothly. "I missed you." Coming down to her, he reached for her hand.

Jessa eluded him, and men with drawn guns came into view. They wore coveralls, fusion-welders' masks, tool belts, and greasy headbands, but they were plainly comfortable with their weapons.

Han shook his head mournfully. "Jess, you've really got me wrong, you'll see." But he knew he had just received an explicit warning, and decided he'd better turn the conversation to the matter at hand. "Where's Doc?"

The scorn left Jessa's features, but she ignored his question. "Come with me, Solo."

Leaving Chewbacca to watch the *Falcon*, Han accompanied her across the temporary base. The landing field was a flat expanse of fusion-formed soil (almost any sort of solid material would do for fusion-forming, Han knew; minerals, vegetable matter, or any old enemies for whom you had no further use). Male, female, human, and nonhuman techs scrambled over vehicles and machinery of every category, aided by a wild assortment of 'droids and other automata, engaged in repair, salvage, and modification.

Han admired the operation as he walked. A tech who'd do illegal work could be found almost anywhere, but Doc, Jessa's father, had an operation that was famous among lawbreakers everywhere. If you wanted your ship repaired without questions as to why you'd been through a firefight, if you needed a vessel's ID profile and appearance changed for reasons best left unmentioned, or if you had a hot piece of major hardware to buy or sell—the person to contact, if you met his rigorous background check, was Doc. If something could be done with machinery, he and his outlaw-techs could do it.

Several of the modifications done on the *Millennium Falcon* had been performed through the outlaw-tech's good offices; he and Han had dealt with each other on a number of occasions. Han admired the shifty old man because he'd been sought by Authority and other official forces for years but never apprehended. Doc had kept himself well buffered, and piped into as many crooked bureaucrats and scuttlebutt sources as anyone Han knew. More than one strike unit had moved against the outlaw-techs only to capture a target area empty of everything but abandoned buildings and useless junk. Doc had joked that he was the only felon in the galaxy who'd have to set up an employee pension plan.

Threading among disassembled hulks and humming repair docks, Jessa led Han through the largest hangar on the base. At one end, slabs of Permex had been joined into a stark cube of an office. But when its door slid up at her command, Han could see that Doc's taste hadn't coarsened. The office featured carpets of Wrodian weave, glittering in rich colors, each one representing generations' work. There were shelves of rare books, lavish hangings, and paintings and sculpture, some by history's greatest artists and others by unknowns who'd simply struck Doc's fancy. There was a monolithic, hand-carved scentwood desk with only one item on it, a holocube of Jessa. In it she was wearing a stylish evening gown, smiling, much more like a pretty girl at her first formal reception than a top-flight outlaw-tech genius.

"Where's the old man?" Han asked, seeing the room was empty. Jessa slid into the conform-lounger behind the desk. She clenched her hands on the lounger's thick, luxurious arms until her fingers made deep indentations.

"He's not here, Solo. Doc's gone."

"How informative; I'd never have guessed it just

from seeing the room's empty. Look, Jess, I have no time for games, no matter how much you'd like to play. I want—"

"I know what you want!" Her face was bitter; it took him by surprise. "No one comes to us unless we know what they want from us. But my father's not here. He's disappeared, and nothing I've tried has turned up a hint. Believe me, Solo, I've tried it all."

Han eased down into a seat across the desk from her. Jessa explained, "Doc went off on one of his buying trips—you know, shopping for stuff that would fit the market, or for some customer's special order. He made three stops and never arrived at the fourth. Just like that. He, three crewmen, and a star yacht just dropped out of sight."

Han thought for a moment about the old man with work-hardened hands, a quick, crusty grin, and a halo of frizzy white hair. Han had liked him, but if Doc was gone, that was that. Few people who vanished under circumstances like that ever showed up again. Luck of the draw. Han had always traveled light, with emotional baggage the first thing he jettisoned, and grief was far too heavy to lug around among the stars.

So that only left thinking, *Goodbye, Doc,* and dealing with Jessa, the old man's only surviving kin. But when his brief distraction broke, he saw that she'd studied the entire play of his thoughts on his face. "You got through that eulogy pretty fast, didn't you, Solo?" she asked softly. "Nobody gets too far under that precious skin of yours, isn't that so?"

That pricked him. "If it was me who'd checked out, would Doc have gone on a crying jag, Jess? Would you? I'm sorry, but life goes on, and if you lose sight of that, sweetheart, you're asking to be dealt out."

Her mouth opened to reply, but she thought better of it and changed tack. Her voice became as sharp as a vibroblade. "Very well. Let's do business. I know what you're looking for, the sensor suite, the dish, the Waiver. I can take care of all of it. We got our hands on a sensor suite, powerful, compact, a military package built for long-range scoutships. It found its way to us from a supply depot; got misrouted by a happy co-incidence I arranged. I can handle the Waiver, too. That only leaves"—she gazed at him coldly—"the question of price."

Han wasn't crazy about the way she'd said it. "The money's got to be right, Jess. I've only got—"

She cut him off again. "Who said money? I know *just* how much you have, high roller, and where you got it, and how much you gave Ploovo. Don't you think we hear everything sooner or later? Would I assume an imbecile who's been gunrunning would be flush?" She leaned back, interlacing her fingers.

He was confused. He'd planned to arrange long terms with Doc, but doubted if he could with Jessa. If she knew he couldn't meet a decent price, why was she talking to him? "Are you going to explain, Jess, or am I supposed to do my famous mind-reading act?"

"Give your jaws a rest, Solo, and pay attention. I'm offering you a deal, a handwash."

He was suspicious, knowing there'd be no generosity from her. But what were his alternatives? He needed his ship repaired, and the rest of it, or he might as well go somewhere out on the galactic rim and bid on a contract to haul garbage. With exaggerated sweetness, he answered, "I'm hanging on your every word. By what, I won't mention."

"It's a pickup, Solo, an extraction. There are details, but that's basically it; you make contact with some people and take them where they want to go, within reason. They won't be expecting you to drop them anywhere risky. Even your stunted attention span ought to suffice for that."

"Where's the pickup?"

"Orron III. That's mostly an agricultural world, except that the Authority has a data center there. That's where your passengers are."

"An Authority Data Center?" Han exploded. "And how do I get into a place like that? It'll look like the Espos' Annual Picnic and Grand Reunion. Listen, toots, I want that stuff from you, but I want to live to a ripe old age, too; I plan to sit in a rocker at the Old

Spacemen's Home, and what you're suggesting will definitely exclude that option."

"It's not so terrible," she replied levelly. "Internal security's not especially bad, because only two types of vessels are cleared to land on Orron III—drone barges for the crops and Authority fleet ships."

"Yeah, but in case you haven't noticed, the *Falcon*'s neither."

"Not yet, Solo, but I'll change that. We have a barge shell, hijacked it in transit. That wasn't much of a trick; they're robot hulks, and they're pretty dumb. I'll fit the *Millennium Falcon* with external control couplings and set her in where the command/control module usually goes, and partition into the hold space. My people can mock up the hull structure so it'll con the Espos, port officials, or anybody else. You land, contact the parties in question, and off you go. Average ground time for a barge is about thirty hours, so you'll have plenty of leeway to get things done. Once you're in transit, you ditch the barge shell and you're home free."

He thought hard about that one. He didn't like anyone messing with his ship. "Why pick me for this thrilling honor? And why the *Falcon*?"

"Because you need something from me, for one thing, so you'll do it. Because, for another, even though you're an amoral mercenary, you're the hottest pilot I know; you've flown everything from a jetpack to a capital ship. As for the *Falcon,* she's just the right size, and has computer capacity to spare, to run the barge. It's a fair deal."

One thing had him puzzled. "Who's the pickup? It sounds like you're going to an awful lot of trouble for them."

"No one you'd know. They're strictly amateurs, and they pay well. What they're doing's no concern of yours, but if they feel like telling you, that's their decision."

He gazed up at the ceiling, which was patterned with glow-pearls. Jessa was offering everything he needed to make the Authority ripe for the plucking.

He could give up gunrunning, petty-cash trips to back-water worlds, all that low-ante stuff.

"Well," coaxed Jessa, "do I tell my techs to get busy, or do you and the Wookiee plan to teach the galaxy the folly of crime by starving in poverty?"

He brought his chair upright. "You better let me break the news to Chewie first, or your wrench jockeys will be nothing but a mound of spare parts for the organ banks."

Doc's organization—now Jessa's—was nothing if not thorough. They had the factory specs for the *Millennium Falcon*, plus complete design holos on every piece of augmentative gear in her. With Chewbacca's help and a small horde of outlaw-techs, Han had the *Falcon*'s engine shielding removed and her control systems exposed in a matter of hours.

Service 'droids trundled back and forth while energy cutters flared, and techs of many races crawled over, under, and into the freighter. It made Han jittery to see so many tools, hands, tentacles, servo-grips, and lift-locks near his beloved ship, but he gritted his teeth and simply did his best to be everywhere at once—and came close to succeeding. Chewbacca covered the things his partner missed, startling any erring tech or 'droid with a high-decibel snarl. No one doubted for a moment what the Wookiee would do to the being or mechanical who damaged the starship.

Han was interrupted by Jessa, who had come up to inspect his progress. With her was an odd-looking 'droid, built along human lines. The machine was rather stocky, shorter than the woman, covered with dents, scrapes, smudges, and spot-welds. Its chest region was unusually broad, and its arms, hanging nearly to its knees, gave it a somewhat simian aspect. Its finish was a flat brown primer job, peeling in places, and it had a stiff, snapping way of moving. The 'droid's red, unblinking photoreceptors trained on Han.

"Meet your passenger," Jessa invited.

Han's features clouded. "You never said anything

about taking a 'droid." He looked at the aged mechanical. "What's he run on, peat?"

"No. And I warned you there'd be details. Bollux here is one of them." She turned to the 'droid. "Okay, Bollux, open up the fruit stand."

"Yes, ma'am," Bollux replied in a leisurely drawl. There was a servomotor hum, and the 'droid's chest plastron split down the center, the halves swinging away to either side. Nestled in among the goodies that were the 'droid's innards was a special emplacement; secured in the emplacement was another unit, a separate machine entity of some kind that was approximately cubical, with several protrusions and folded appendages. Atop it was a photoreceptor mount, monocular lensed. The unit was painted in deep, protective, multilayered blue. The monocular came on, lighting red.

"Say hello to Captain Solo, Max," Jessa instructed it.

The machine-within-a-machine studied Han up and down, photoreceptor angling and swiveling. "Why?" it demanded. The pitch of its vocal mechanism was like that of a child.

Jessa countered frankly, "Because if you don't, Max, the nice man is liable to chuck your teensy iron behind out into deep space—that's why."

"Hello!" chirped Max, with what Han suspected to be forced cheer. "A great pleasure to make your acquaintance, Captain!"

"The parties you're picking up need to collect and withdraw data from the computer system on Orron III," Jessa explained. "Of course, they couldn't just ask the Authority there for probe equipment without raising suspicions, and your walking in with Max under your arm might cause a few problems, too. But nobody's going to bother much about an old labor 'droid. We named him Bollux because we had so many headaches restructuring his gut. We never did get his vocal pattern up to speed.

"Anyway, that cutie in Bollux's chest cavity is Blue Max; Max because we crammed as much computer

42

capacity into him as we could, and blue for reasons that even you, Solo, can see, I'm sure. Blue Max was a piece of work, even for us. He's puny, but he cost plenty, even though he's immobile and we had to leave out a lot of the usual accessories. But he's all they'll need to tap that data system."

Han was studying the two machines, hoping Jessa would admit she'd been joking. He'd seen weirder gizmos in his time, but never on a passenger roster. He didn't like 'droids very much, but decided he could live with these.

He bent down for a better squint at Blue Max. "You stay in there all the time?"

"I can function autonomously or in linkage," Max squeaked.

"Fabulous," Han said dryly. He tapped Bollux's head. "Button up." As the brown segments of plastron swung shut on Max, Han called up to Chewbacca, "Yo, partner, find a place and stow this mollusk, will you? He's with us." He turned back to Jessa. "Anything else? A marching band, maybe?"

She never did get to answer. Just then klaxons went off, sirens began to warble at deafening levels, and the public-address horns started paging her to the base's command post. Everywhere in the hangar, outlaw-techs dropped their tools in a ringing barrage and dashed off frantically for emergency stations. Jessa sprinted away instantly. Han took off after her, yelling back for Chewbacca to stay with their ship.

The two crossed the complex. Humans, nonhumans, and machines charged in every direction, necessitating a good deal of dodging and swerving. The command post was a simple bunker, but at the bottom of the steps leading to it, Jessa and Han entered a well-equipped, fully manned operations room. A giant holo-tank dominated the room with its phantom light, an analogue of the solar system around them. Sun, planets, and other major astronomical bodies were picked out in keyed colors.

"Sensors have painted an unidentified blip, Jessa," said one of the duty officers, pointing out a yellow speck at the edge of the system. "We're awaiting positive ID."

She bit her lip, eyes fastened to the tank along with those of all the others in the bunker. Han moved up next to her. The speck was moving toward the center of the holotank, which would be, Han knew, the planet on which he was standing, represented by a bead of white light. The bogie's speed decreased, and sensors painted a cluster of smaller blips breaking away from it. Then the original object accelerated, kept on accelerating, and faded from the tank a moment later.

"It was an Authority fleet ship, a corvette," the officer said. "It launched a flight of fighters, four of them, then ducked back into hyperspace. It must've detected us and gone for help, leaving the fighters to harass and keep us busy until it can return. I don't see how they happened to be searching this system."

Han realized the officer was looking directly at him. In fact, everybody in the command post was, and hands had gone to side arms. "Whoa, Jess," he protested, meeting her eyes, "when did I ever stooge for the Espos?"

For a moment an expression of uncertainty crossed her face, but only for a moment. "I guess if you'd tipped them you wouldn't have stuck around while they dropped in," she admitted. "Besides, they would have shown up in full strength if they'd known we were here. You've got to concede, though, Solo, it's some coincidence."

He changed the subject. "Why didn't the corvette just put through a hyperspace transmission? They must be close enough to a base to call for support."

"This area's full of stellar anomalies," she said absently, focusing back on those ominous blips. "It fouls up hyperspace commo; that's why we picked it, partly. What's the fighters' estimated time of arrival?" she asked the officer.

"ETA less than twenty minutes," was the reply.

She blew her breath out. "And we haven't got anything combatworthy except fighters ourselves. No use

44

ducking it; get ready to scramble. Order evacuation to start in the meantime."

She looked to Han. "Those are probably IRDs; they'll eat up anything I can send up right now except for some old snubs I have here. I need to buy time, and I have almost nobody who's done any combat flying. Will you help?"

He saw all the graves faces still staring at him. He led Jessa to one side, caressed her cheek, but spoke in a low tone. "My darling Jess, this definitely was *not* in our deal. I'm for the Old Spacemen's Home, remember? I have no intention of ever plunking my rear into one of those suicide sleds again."

Her voice was eloquent. "There are lives at stake! We can't evacuate in time, even if we leave everything behind. I'll send up inexperienced pilots if it comes to that, but they'll be cold meat for those Espo flyers. You've got more experience than all the rest of us put together!"

"All of which cries out to me that there's no percentage fighting the good fight," he parried, but he burned from the look she gave him. He nearly spoke again but held his tongue, unable to untangle his own nagging ambiguities.

"Then go hide," she said so low he could barely hear, "but you can forget your precious *Millennium Falcon,* Solo, because there's no power in the universe that can make her spaceworthy before those raiders hit us and pin us down. And once their reinforcements arrive, they'll carve this base and everything in it to atoms!"

His ship, of course; that's what must have been biting at the back of my mind, Han told himself. Must have been. The turbo-laser cannon would never stop fast, evasive fighters, and the raiders would indeed take the base apart. He and Chewbacca might possibly escape with their lives, but without their ship they'd be just two nameless, homeless pieces of interstellar flotsam.

In the confusion of the command post, with the giving and receiving of frantic messages, she still heard his voice among all the others.

"Jess?" She stared, confused, at his lopsided smirk. "Got a flight helmet for me?" He pretended not to see the sudden softening of her expression. "Something sporty, in my size, Jess, with a hole in it to match the one in my head."

☐IV

HAN tagged after Jessa in another quick run across the base. They entered one of the lesser hangar domes where the air was filled with the whine of high-performance engines. Six fighters were parked there, their ground crews attending them, checking out power levels, armaments, deflectors, and control systems.

The fighters were primarily for interceptor service—or rather, Han corrected himself, had been a generation ago. They were early production snubships; Z-95 Headhunters; compact, twin-engined swing-wing craft. Their fuselages, wings and forked tails were daubed with the drab spots, smears, and spray-splotches of general camouflage coats. Their external hardpoints, where rockets and bomb pylons had once been mounted, were now bare.

Indicating the snubs, Han asked Jessa, "What'd you do, knock over a museum?"

"Picked them up from a planetary constabulary; they were using them for antismuggling operations, matter of fact. We worked them over for resale, but hung on to them because they're the only combat craft we've got right now. And don't be so condescending, Solo; you've spent your share of time in snubs."

That he had. Han dashed over to one of the Head-hunters as a ground crewman finished fueling it. He took a high leap and chinned himself on the lip of the cockpit to eyeball it. Most of its console panels had been removed in the course of years of repair, leaving linkages and wiring exposed. The cockpit was just as cramped as he remembered.

But with that, the Z-95 Headhunter was still a good little ship, legendary for the amount of punishment it could soak up. Its pilot's seat—the "easy chair," in parlance—was set back at a thirty-degree angle to help offset gee-forces, the control stick built into its armrest. He let himself back down.

Several pilots had already gathered there, and another, a humanoid, showed up just then. There was little enough worry on their faces that Han concluded they hadn't flown combat before. Jessa came up beside him and pressed an old, lusterless bowl of a flight helmet into his hands.

"Who's flown one of these beasts before?" he asked as he tried the helmet on. It was a bad fit, too tight. He began pulling at the webbing adjustment tabs in its sweat-stained interior.

"We've all been up," one pilot answered, "to practice basic tactics."

"Oh, fine," he muttered, trying the helmet on again. "We'll rip 'em apart up there." The headgear was still too tight. With an impatient click of her tongue, Jessa took it from him and began working on it herself.

He addressed his temporary command. "The Authority's got newer ships; they can afford to buy whatever they want. That fighter spread coming in at us is probably made up of IRD ships straight off the government inventory, maybe prototypes, maybe production models. And the guys flying those IRDs learned how at an academy. I suppose it'd be too much to hope that anybody here has even been to one?"

It was. Han went on, raising his voice over the increasing engine noise. "IRD fighters have an edge in speed, but these old Headhunters can make a tighter turn and take a real beating, which is why they're still around. IRDs aren't very aerodynamic, that's their nature. Their pilots hate to come down and lock horns

47

in a planetary atmosphere; they call it *goo*. These boys'll have to, though, to hit the base, but we can't wait until they get down here to hit them, or some might get through.

"We've got six ships. That's three two-ship elements. If you've got anything worth protecting with those flight helmets, you'll remember this: stay with your wing man. Without him, you're dead. Two ships together are five times as effective as they would be alone, and they're ten times safer."

The Z-95s were ready now, and the IRDs' arrival not far off. Han had a thousand things to tell these green flyers, but how could he give them a training course in minutes? He knew he couldn't.

"I'll make this simple. Keep your eyes open and make sure it's your guns, not your tail, that's pointed at the enemy. Since we're protecting a ground installation, we'll have to ride our kills. That means if you're not sure whether the opposition is hit or faking, you sit on his tail and make sure he goes down and stays down. Don't think just because he's nosediving and leaving a vapor trail that he's out of it. That's an old trick. If you get an explosion from him, fine. If you get a flamer, let him go; he's finished. But otherwise you ride your kill all the way down to the cellar. We've got too much to lose here."

He made that last remark thinking of the *Falcon*, shutting out human factors, telling himself his ship was the reason he was about to hang his hide out in the air. Strictly business.

Jessa had thrust his helmet into his hands. He tried it on again; it was a perfect fit. He turned to say thanks and noticed for the first time that she was carrying a flight helmet, too.

"Jess, no. Absolutely not."

She sniffed. "They're my ships, in the first place. Doc taught me everything; I've been flying since I was five. And who d'you think taught these others the basics? Besides, there's no one else even nearly qualified."

"Training exercises are different!" Of all things, he

didn't want to have to worry about her up there. "I'll get Chewie; he's done some—"

"Oh, brilliant, Solo! We can just build a dormer onto the canopy bubble and that hyperthyroid dust-mop of yours can fly the ship with his kneecaps!"

Han resigned himself to the fact that she was the logical one to fly. She turned to her other pilots. "Solo's right; this one'll be a toughie. We don't want to engage them out in space, because all the advantages out there are theirs, but we don't want to let them get too close to the surface, either. Our ground defenses couldn't cope with a fighter spread. So somewhere in the middle we'll have to draw the line, depending on how they play it when they come at us. If we can buy time, the ground personnel will have a chance to complete evacuation."

She turned to Han. "Including the *Falcon*. I gave orders to finish her and close her up as soon as possible. I had to divert men to do it, but a deal's a deal. And I sent word to Chewie what's happened."

She pulled her helmet on. "Han's flight leader. I'll assign wing men. Let's move."

With high screeches the six Z-95 Headhunters, like so many mottled arrowheads, sped off into the sky. Han pulled down and adjusted his tinted visor. He checked his weapons again, three blaster cannons in each wing. Satisfied, he maneuvered so that his wing man was above and behind him, relative to the plane of ascent. Seated in his sloped-back easy chair, situated high in the canopy bubble, he had something near 360-degrees' visibility, one of the things he liked most about these old Z-95s.

His wing man was a lanky, soft-spoken young man. Han hoped the guy wouldn't forget to stick close when The Show started.

He thought, *The Show—fighter-pilot jargon.* He'd never thought he'd be using it again, with his blood up and a million things to keep track of, including allies, enemies, and his own ship. And anything that went wrong could bow him out of The Show for good.

Besides, The Show was the province of youth. A fighter could hold only so much gee-compensation equipment, enough to lessen simple linear stress and get to a target or scrap in a hurry, but not enough to offset the punishment of tight maneuvering and sudden acceleration. Dogfighting remained the testing ground of young reflexes, resilience, and coordination.

Once, Han had lived, eaten, and slept high-speed flying. He'd trained under men who thought of little else. Even off-duty life had revolved around hand-eye skills, control, balance. Drunk, he'd stood on his head and played ring-toss, and been flung aloft from a blanket with a handful of darts to twist in midair and throw bull's-eyes time and again. He'd flown ships like this one, and ships a good deal faster, through every conceivable maneuver.

Once. Han was by no means old, but he hadn't been in this particular type of contest for a long time. The flight of Headhunters was pulling itself into two-ship elements, and he found his hands had steadied.

They drew their ships' wings back to minimize drag, wing camber adjusting automatically, and rose at high boost. They would meet their opposition at the edge of space.

"Headhunter leader," he announced over the commo net, "to Headhunter flight. Commo check."

"Headhunter two to leader, in." That was Han's wing man.

"Headhunter three, check," sang Jessa's clear alto.

"Headhunter four, all correct." That had been Jessa's wing man, the gray-skinned humanoid from Lafra who, Han had noticed, had vestiges of soaring membranes, suggesting that he had superior flying instincts and a fine grasp of spacial relationships. The Lafrarian, it had turned out, had over four minutes' actual combat time, which was a good sign. A good many fighter pilots were weeded out in the first minute or so of combat.

Headhunters five and six chimed in, two of Jessa's grease slingers who were brothers to boot. It had been inevitable that they'd be wing men; they'd tend to stick together, and if paired with anyone else, would have been distracted anyway.

Ground control came up. "Headhunter flight, you should have a visual on your opposition within two minutes."

Han had his flight tighten up their ragged formation. "Stay in pairs. If the bandits offer a head-on pass, take them up on it; you can pitch just as hard as they can." He thought it better not to mention that the other side had a longer reach, however.

He had Five and Six, the brothers, drop far back to field any enemies that might break through. The two remaining elements spread out as much as they could without risking separation. Their sensors and those of the approaching ships identified one another, and complex countermeasures and distortion systems switched on. Han knew this engagement would be conducted on visual ranging; all the complicated sensor-warfare apparatus tended to cancel out, no longer to be trusted.

Short-range screens painted four blips. "Go to Heads-Up Displays," Han ordered, and they all cut in their holographics. Transparent projections of their instrumentation hung before them in the canopy bubbles, freeing them of the need to divert their eyes and attention from the task of flying in order to take a reading.

"Here they come!" someone shouted. "At one-zero-slash-two-five!"

The enemy ships were IRD models all right, with bulbous fuselages and the distinctive engine package that characterized that latest military design. They were IRD prototypes. As Han watched, the raiders broke formation into two elements of two ships each in perfect precision.

"Elements break!" he called. "Take 'em!" He led his wing man off to starboard to face that brace of IRDs as Jessa and her humanoid wing man banked to port.

The net came alive with cries of warning. The Espo flyers had disdained evasionary tactics, coming head-on, meaning they were out to put some blood on the

51

walls. Their orders, Han thought, must've been to hit the outlaw-techs as hard as they could.

The IRDs began firing from extreme range with yellow-green flashes of the energy cannon in their chin pods. Deflector shields were up. Han ground his teeth, his hand tight on the stick, disciplining himself not to fire until it could do some good. He fought the urge to rubberneck and see how his other element was doing; each two-ship pair was on its own for the moment. He could only hope everybody would hold together, because the pilot who became a straggler in a row like this seldom came out of it.

Han and the opposing wing leader squared off and bore in on each other. Their wing men, keeping out of the way, were too busy holding position and adapting to their leaders' actions to do any shooting.

The IRD's beams began to make hits, rocking the smaller Headhunter. Han came within range and still held his fire; he had a feeling about this one. The IRD pilot might not even be sure about the old Z-95's reach, but Han suspected he knew what the man would do as soon as he returned fire. Riding the jolting Headhunter through the hail of incoming shots, he bided his time and hoped his shields would hold.

He played it for as long as he dared, only a matter of an extra moment or two, but precious time and vital distance. He let one quick burst go. As he'd suspected, the enemy never intended to face off to the very end. The IRD rolled onto its back, still firing, and Han had the snap shot he'd hoped for. But the IRD fighter was into his gunsight ring and out again like a wraith, so although he scored, Han knew he hadn't done it any damage. The Authority ships were even faster than he'd thought.

Then all bets were off because, despite everything taught in classrooms, the IRDs split up, the wing man peeling away in an abrupt bank. Han's wing man went after him, exclaiming excitedly, "I'm on him!" Han hollered for him to come back and not throw away the security of a two-ship element.

The IRD leader swept by underneath Han. He

knew what that meant, too; the enemy was almost certain to split-S, loop under, and try for a tail position—the kill position. What Han should have done with the slower Headhunter was to fire-wall the throttle and go for clear space until he knew what was what. But the interchange of chatter between Jessa and her wing mate told him that the other pair of IRDs had split up as well, drawing her and her companion out of their pairing.

Han sent his Headhunter into a maximum-performance climbing turn, trying to look everywhere at once, still yelling to his wing man, "Stick with me! They're baiting you!" But he was ignored.

The IRD leader he'd shot at hadn't split-S. The raiders' whole strategy of drawing the defenders out of formation was clear now, too late. The IRD leader had half rolled again, half looped, and come around onto the tail of Han's wing man. The other IRD, the bait, was already racing on toward the backup element, Headhunters five and six. One of the IRDs Jessa had faced joined that one in a new two-ship element.

The Espos had counted on the inexperienced outlaw-techs' breaking formation, Han thought. If we'd stayed together we'd have mopped the floor with them. "Jess, dammit, we've been robbed," he called as he came around, but Jessa had her own troubles. Because she and her wing mate had become separated, an IRD had found the opportunity to fasten itself on her tail.

Han saw that his own wing man was in trouble, but just didn't have the speed to intervene. The IRD leader had attached himself to the Headhunter in the kill position, and the lanky young outlaw-tech was pleading, "Help me, somebody! Get him off me!"

Still way out of range, Han fired anyway, hoping to shake up the IRD leader's concentration. But the enemy was steady and undistracted. He waited until he had the Headhunter perfectly set up and hit the firing button on his control grips in a brief burst. The Z-95 was caught by a yellow-green blast and vanished in a nimbus of white-hot gas and debris.

What Han should have done was draw his remaining ships together in a weaving, mutually protective string or circle. But even as he breathed profanities to himself, he cut a course for the victorious IRD, his blood up, caution forgotten, thinking, *Nobody gets into me for a wing man, pal. Nobody.*

It came to him that he didn't even know that lanky boy's name.

Jessa's wing man, the Lafrarian, shouted, "Scissor right, Headhunter three! Scissor!"

Jessa broke right in a flurry of evasive maneuvers while lines of destruction probed for her. She poured on all speed as her wing man came in at a sharp angle, decreasing his own velocity so that Jessa and her pursuer came across his vector. The Lafrarian settled calmly into the kill position, quickened up, and opened fire.

Lines of red blaster-cannon fire broke from the trailing Headhunter's wings. The raider ship shuddered as pieces of its fuselage were sheared off. There was an explosion, and the crippled IRD went into a helpless flutter, as if it were dragging a broken wing. It began its long fall toward the planet, sentenced to death by simple gravity.

Far below, Headhunters five and six, the two brothers, had engaged the IRDs that had broken through. Off in the distance Han Solo and the IRD leader swept and wove through the permutations of close combat, making their statements in beams of devastation in red, in green.

But Jessa knew where priorities lay, and Five and Six were her weakest flyers. Even now they were calling for help. She and her humanoid wing man closed and sped off to rejoin the fray.

A raider was glued to Headhunter five's tail, chopping at it and holding position through all the insane turns and evasions, refusing to be unseated. The outlaw-tech shoved his stick up into the corner for a pushover but was too slow. The IRD's beams sliced through his ship, depressurizing it and severing him at the waist. The IRD turned toward the other brother,

Headhunter six, as its companion raced on toward the planet and its outlaw base.

Just then Jessa and her wing man arrived, calling for Headhunter six to come under their cover.

"I can't; I'm latched!" the man answered. The IRD that had remained behind had come out of a smooth barrel roll and attached itself to him. Jessa's wing man threw himself in to help and she came right behind. The sliding, jockeying string of four ships plunged toward the planet's surface.

The IRD made its kill a moment later. Headhunter six split apart in a blossom of fire and wreckage just as its killer came under Jessa's wing man's guns.

The Espo flyer applied more of his ship's amazing speed to improve his lead and came up as if he were going into a loop, making the Lafrarian misjudge. The IRD flashed out of the maneuver instead, in a lightning-fast turn, banked, and managed to make a high deflection shot.

The IRD's cannon scored, and her wing man's Headhunter shook as Jessa raised her voice in alarm, sheering off as quickly as she could. She banked and sensed a shadow near. The IRD swooped past. She swerved and shot at it instinctively. The burst scored, penetrating the IRD's shields. As the IRD dropped away in an emergency power dive, its pilot struggling to adjust his craft's thrust bias and avert disaster, Jessa ignored Han's dictum that she ride her kill. She returned to see what she could do for her wing mate.

Exactly nothing. The Lafrarian's ship was damaged but not in danger of crashing. He'd put it into a shallow glide, extending his wings to their fullest.

"Can you make it?"

"Yes, Jessa. But at least one of the IRD has gotten through. The other may manage to rejoin him."

"Nurse your ship back. I've got to get down there."

"Good hunting, Jessa!"

She opened her ship's engines in a power dive.

Han found out right away that the IRD leader was

a good pilot. He discovered it by nearly getting his easy chair shot out from underneath him.

The Espo flyer was hot, accurate with his weaponry, deft with his maneuvers. He and Han quickly joined in circling, pouncing, cloverleaf battle, the upper hand alternating between them. Rolling, looping, doing their best to turn inside each other's turns, sliding into and out of each other's gunsights over and over, they never let their sticks sit still for an instant.

For the third time Han shook the IRD off, playing on his Headhunter's greater maneuverability against the IRD's superior speed. He watched the Espo flyer try to pick him up again. "I guess you must be the local champ, huh?" The IRD came at him once more. "Have it your way, bozo. Let's see what you've really got."

He split-S down deeper into the planet's atmosphere as the IRD sprang at his tail, gaining in the descent but unable to hold the Headhunter in his sights. Han pulled up sharply, twisted his ship into a half loop, flipped over, and went into a diving aileron roll with another loop thrown in, coming out of the combo in the opposite direction.

Cannon blasts streaked by over the canopy bubble, barely missing. Man, this Espo can really *latch*, Han told himself. But he has a few things left to learn. School ain't over yet.

He rammed the stick into the corner for a pushover and began a power dive. The IRD hung in but couldn't quite draw a bead on him. Han pushed the Headhunter to its limits, ducking and slipping as the Espo pilot raked at him. The snub's engines moaned, and every particle of her vibrated as if desiring to fly apart. Han jostled, watching his Heads-Up Display for the reading he wanted. The IRD's shots ranged closer.

Then he had it. He began pulling out of his dive, nosing up slowly and dreading the shot from behind that would end all his problems and hopes.

But the IRD pilot held off, not wanting to waste the opportunity, waiting for the Headhunter to present a spread-eagled silhouette in his gunsight. Han thought, *Sure, he wants this one to be the perfect kill.*

He yanked into a turn as the IRD aligned itself, trailing him into it and edging for a lead. Han cheated the turn tighter, and tighter yet. But the IRD pilot clung doggedly, to end the frustrating chase and prove who was the hotter pilot.

And then Han had the turn tighter than ninety degrees, the thing he'd been working toward all along. The Espo hadn't paid enough attention to his altimeter, and now the thicker air was working against the IRD, cutting down on its performance. It couldn't hold a turn this tight.

And just as the IRD broke off its run, Han, with the instincts that had given him a reputation for telepathy, threw his Headhunter into a vertical reversement. The IRD was close enough now. Han fired a sustained burst and the IRD became a cloud of light, throwing out glowing motes and bits of wreckage in every direction.

And as the Headhunter zipped past the showering remains of its opponent, Han crowed, "Happy graduation day, *sucker!*"

The fourth IRD had already made three strafing runs on the outlaw-tech base. The base's defensive guns couldn't keep up with it; they'd been set up for actions against large ships and mass assault, not agile, low-angle fighter attacks.

The raider had concentrated on flak suppression for his first runs. Now most of the gun emplacements were silent. Outlaws dead and dying lay in a base where several buildings were already holed or ablaze.

Then Jessa showed up. Maintaining the velocity she'd picked up in her dive, ignoring the fact that the wings might be ripped off her stubborn little Headhunter at any moment, she threw herself after the IRD just as it came out of its pass. Those people down there were hers, were suffering and perishing because they worked for her. She was absolutely adamant that no more runs would be made at them.

But as she was lining up on the IRD a volley of

cannon fire sizzled down from above, nipping at the leading edge of her starboard wing. Another IRD flashed by with speed it had picked up in its own dive, the ship she had thought to be disabled. Its shots had penetrated her shields and come close to cleaving her wing.

But she held position, determined to get at least one of the raiders before they got her.

Then the second IRD itself became a target. Han had it in his sights for an instant in a side-on, high deflection shot. He jinxed the nose of his ship, laying out sleeper rounds ahead of the Espo, investing in the future. It paid off; the IRD vanished in an outlashing of force and shrapnel.

"You're on the last one, Jess!" he informed her in a crackle of static. "Swat him!"

She was lined on the IRD again. She fired, but only her portside cannon worked; the damage to her starboard wing had knocked out its guns. Her target being slightly off to starboard, she missed.

The IRD began surging ahead, capitalizing on its raw ion power, slipping away to starboard. In another split second it would get away. Jessa snap-rolled, sliding to starboard belly-up, and fired again. Her remaining guns reached out with red fingers of destruction and hit. The IRD flared and flamed, breaking apart.

"Nice shooting, doll," Han called over the net. Jessa's Headhunter continued along, canopy lowermost, not far from the ground. He cut in full power and went after her, saying, "Jess, in aerospace circles, what we call what you are is upside down."

"I can't get back over!" There was desperation in her tone. "That damage I took must've started a burnout creepage. My controls are dead!"

He was about to instruct her to punch out but stopped himself. She was too close to the surface; her ejection seat would never have time to right itself. Her ship was losing altitude rapidly. Only seconds were left.

He swept in and matched speeds with her. "Jess, get ready to go when I give you the word."

She was mystified. What could he mean? She was dead, crashing or ejecting. But she prepared to do as he said. Han eased the wing of his Headhunter under her overturned one. She saw his plan and her breath caught in her throat.

"On three," he told her. *"One!"* On that count he brought his wing tip up under hers. *"Two!"* They both felt the jar of hazardous contact, knowing the most miniscule mistake would strew them both all over the flat landscape.

Han rolled left, and the ground that had been streaking by beneath Jessa's dangling head seemed to rotate away as Han's Headhunter imparted spin to hers. He finished his roll with additional force.

"Three! Punch out, Jess!" He himself was fighting to keep his jostled ship from going out of control.

But before he'd even said half of it, she'd gone, her canopy bubble propelled up and back by separator charges, her ejection seat—the easy chair—flung high and clear of her descending ship. The Headhunter plowed into the planet's surface, making a long strip of fiery ruin along the ground, becoming the day's final casualty.

Jessa watched from her ejection seat while its repulsor units steadied and eased her down toward the ground on gusts of power. Off in the distance, she could see her Lafrarian wing man nursing his damaged craft in for a landing.

Han maneuvered his Headhunter through a long turn, coaxing with his retrothrusters until he was at a near stall. He brought his ship down nearby just as Jessa touched down.

The bubble popped up. He removed his helmet and jumped out of the aged fighter just as she slid free of her harness and threw her own helmet aside, feeling around and finding herself generally whole.

Han sauntered over, stripping off his flying gloves. "There's room for two in my ship if we squeeze," he leered.

"As I live and breathe," she scoffed. "Have we finally seen Han Solo do something unselfish? Are you going soft? Who knows, you may even pick up a little morality one day, if you ever wake up and get wise to yourself."

He stopped, his leer gone. He glared at her for a moment, then said, "I already know all about morality, Jess. A friend of mine made a decision once, thought he was doing the moral thing. Hell, he *was*. But he'd been conned. He lost his career, his girl, everything. This friend of mine, he ended up standing there while they ripped the rank and insignia off his tunic. The people who didn't want him put up against a wall and shot were laughing at him. A whole planet. He shipped out of there and never went back."

She watched his face become ugly. "Wouldn't anyone testify for—your friend?" she asked softly.

He sniggered. "His commanding officer committed perjury against him. There was only one witness in his defense, and who's going to believe a Wookiee?"

He fended off her next remark by glancing at the base. "Looks like they never touched the main hangar. You can have the *Falcon* finished in no time and still evacuate before the Espos show up. Then I'll be on my way. We've both got things to do."

She closed one eye, looking at him sidelong. "It's lucky I know you're a mercenary, Solo. It's lucky I know you only flew that Headhunter to protect the *Falcon,* not to protect lives. And that you saved me so I could hold up my end of our bargain. It's lucky you'll probably never do a single selfless, decent thing in your life, and that everything that happened today fits in, in some crazy way, with that greedy, retarded behavioral pattern of yours."

He stared at her quizzically. "Lucky?"

She started for his fighter, walking tiredly. "Lucky for me," Jessa said over her shoulder.

V

"WHAT'D you say, Bollux? Quit whispering!"

Han, seated across the gameboard from Chewbacca, glared at a crate on the other side of the *Millennium Falcon*'s forward compartment, where the old 'droid sat. The compartment's other clutter included shipping containers, pressure kegs, insulated canisters, and spare parts.

The Wookiee, seated on the acceleration couch, chin resting on one enormous paw, studied the holographic game pieces. His eyes were narrowed in concentration and his black snout twitched from time to time. He'd spotted Han two pieces, and was now on the verge of wiping out that advantage. The pilot had been playing poorly, his concentration wandering, fretting and preoccupied with the complications of the voyage. The new sensor package and dish were working perfectly, and the starship's systems had been fine-tuned by the outlaw-techs. Nevertheless, Han's mind couldn't rest easy as long as his cherished *Falcon* was hooked up to the huge barge like a bug on a bladderbird. Furthermore, the trip was taking far longer than the *Falcon* alone would have required; the barge wasn't built for speed.

Han could hear the barge's engines now, their muffled blast vibrating through the freighter's deck and his boots, into the soles of his feet. He hated that barge, wished he could just dump it and zoom off; but a bargain was, after all, a bargain. And, as Jessa had explained, the Waiver for the *Falcon* was being arranged by the people he was to pick up on Orron III, so it behooved him to hold up his end of the agreement.

"I didn't say anything, sir," Bollux replied politely. "That was Max."

"Then what did *he* say?" Han snapped. The two-in-one machines sometimes communicated between themselves by high-speed informational pulses, but seemed to prefer vocal-mode conversations. It always made Han nervous when Bollux's chest was closed up, with the diminutive computer's voice rising spectrally from an unseen source.

"He informed me, Captain," Bollux replied in his slow fashion, "that he would like me to open my plastron. May I?"

Han, who'd turned back to the gameboard, saw that Chewbacca had sprung a clever trap. While his finger hovered indecisively over the programming keys controlling his pieces, Han muttered, "Sure, sure, go on, you can fan the air for all I care, Bollux." He scowled at the Wookiee, seeing there was no way out of the trap. Chewbacca threw his head back with a toss of red-brown hair and woofed with laughter, showing jutting fangs.

With a soft hiss of escaping air—his plastron was airtight, insulated, and shockproof—Bollux's chest swung open as the labor 'droid moved his long arms back out of the way. Blue Max's monocular came alive and tracked over to the gameboard just as Han punched up his next move. His gamepiece, a miniature, three-dimensional monster, jumped into battle with one of Chewie's. But Han had misjudged the two pieces' subtle win-lose parameters. The Wookiee's simulacrum-beastie won the brief fight. Han's gamepiece evaporated back into the nothingness of computer modeling from which it had come.

"You should have used the Second Ilthmar Defense," Blue Max volunteered brightly. Han swung around with murder in his eye; even the precocious Max recognized the look, hastily adding, "Only trying to be of assistance, sir."

"Blue Max is quite new, quite young, Captain,"

Bollux supplied, by way of mollifying Han. "I've taught him a bit about the board game, but he doesn't know much yet about human sensitivities."

"Is that so?" Han asked, as if fascinated. "So who's teaching him, Mr. Pick and Shovel, you?"

"Sure," Max bubbled. "Bollux's been *everywhere*. We sit and talk all the time, and he tells me about the places he's seen."

Han swiped at the gameboard's master key, clearing it of his defeated holo-beasties and Chewbacca's victorious ones. "Do tell? Well, now, that must be some kind of education: *Slit Trenches I Have Dug— a Trans-Galactic Diary*."

"The great starship yards of Fondor was where I was activated," Bollux responded, in his slow way. "Then, for a time, I worked for a planetary survey Alpha-Team, and after that, for a construction gang on weather-control systems. I had a job as general roustabout for Gan Jan Rue's Traveling Menagerie, and as maintenance helper in the Trigdale Foundaries. And more. But one by one, the jobs have been taken over by newer models. I volunteered for all the modifications and reprogramming I could, but eventually I simply couldn't compete with the newer, more capable 'droids."

Interested now despite himself, Han asked, "How'd Jessa pick you for this ride?"

"She didn't, sir; I requested it. There was word that a 'droid would be selected from the general labor pool for some unstated modification. I was there, having been purchased at open auction. I went to her and asked if I might be of use."

Han chortled. "And for that they yanked out part of you, rearranged the rest, and stuck that coin bank inside you. You call that a deal?"

"It has its disadvantages, sir. But it's kept me functioning at a relatively high level of activity. There would probably have been some lesser vacancy for me elsewhere, Captain, even if it were only shoveling biological byproducts on a nontechnological world, but at least I have avoided obsolescence for the time being."

Han gaped at the 'droid, wondering if he were circuit-crazy. "So what, Bollux? What's the point? You're not your own master. You don't even have a say in your own name; you have to reprogram to whatever your new owner decides to call you, and 'Bollux' is a joke. Eventually you'll be of no further use, and then it's Scrap City."

Chewbacca was listening intently now. He was far older than any human, and his perspectives were different from a man's . . . or a 'droid's. Bollux's leisurely speech made him sound serene as he replied, "Obsolescence for a 'droid, sirs, is much like death for a human, or a Wookiee. It is the end of function, which means the end of significance. So it is to be avoided at all costs, in my opinion, Captain. After all, what value is there to existence without purpose?"

Han jumped to his feet, mad without knowing exactly why, except that he felt dumb for arguing with a junk-heap 'droid. He decided to tell Bollux just what a deluded, misfit chump the old labor 'droid really was.

"Bollux, do you know what you are?"

"Yessir, a smuggler, sir," Bollux responded promptly.

Han, confused, looked at the 'droid for a moment, his mouth hanging open, taken off balance by the reply. Even a labor 'droid ought to recognize a rhetorical question, he thought. *"What* did you say?"

"I said, 'Yessir, a smuggler, sir,' " Bollux drawled, "like yourself. One who engages in the illegal import or export of"—his metal forefinger pointed down at Blue Max, nestled in his thorax—"concealed goods."

Chewbacca, paws clasped to his stomach, was rolling around on the acceleration couch, laughing in hysterical grunts, kicking his feet in the air.

Han's temper blew. "Shut up!" he shouted at the 'droid. Bollux, again with that strange literalness, obediently swung his chest panels closed. Chewbacca's laughter had him close to suffocation, as tears appeared around his tight-shut eyes. Han began looking around for a wrench or a hammer, or another instrument of technological mayhem, not intending to have any 'droid one-up him and survive to tell the tale. But at that moment the navicomputer bleeped an alert. Han and Chewbacca instantly charged for the cockpit, the Wookiee still clasping his midsection, to prepare for reversion to normal space.

The tedious trip to Orron III had gnawed at their nerves; both pilot and copilot were grateful for the reappearance of stars that marked emergence from hyperspace, though it was accompanied by a wallowing of the gigantic barge shell. The barge's ovoid hull bulged beneath them, a metal can of a ship with a minimum of engine power. Jessa's techs had executed their hull mock-up so that the *Falcon*'s cockpit retained most of its field of vision.

Han and Chewbacca kept their hands off the ship's controls, letting the computer do the work, maintaining the role of an automated barge. The automatics accepted their landing instructions, and the composite ship began its ungainly descent through the atmosphere.

Orron III was a planet generous to man, its axial tilt negligible, its seasons stable and, throughout most of its latitudes, conducive to good crop production, and its soil rich and fertile. The Authority had recognized the planet's potential as a bread basket and wasted no time in taking advantage of its year-round growing season. Since the planet had more than adequate resources, room, and a strategic location, they had opted to build a data center there as well, thus simplifying logistics and security for both operations.

Orron III was undeniably beautiful, wreathed with strings and strands of white cloud systems, and showing the soft greens and blues of abundant plant life and broad oceans. As they made their approach, Han and Chewbacca ran sensor readings, taking the layout of the Authority installations.

"What was that?" Han asked, leaning forward for a closer look at his instruments. The Wookiee wooffed uncertainly. "I thought I caught something for a second, big blip in a slow transpolar orbit, but either it went around the planet's horizon or we've dropped too low to pick it up. Or both." He worried about it for a moment, then firmly instructed himself not to borrow trouble; whether or not there was a picket ship should make no difference.

Ground features began to resolve into gently rolling country divided precisely into the huge parcels of individual fields. The various shades of those fields reflected a wide range of crops at various states of maturity. Planting, growing, and harvesting must be done on a rolling basis on a large agriworld, for optimal utilization of equipment and manpower.

Eventually they could discern the spaceport, a kilometers-wide stretch of landing area built to the immense proportions of the great robo-barges. The main part of the port, which supported the Authority fleet ships, occupied only a small corner of the installation, even taking into consideration its communications and housing complexes. The majority of the place was simply mooring space for the barges, abysslike berths where maintenance gantries could reach them for repair work and the lumbering mobile silos, aided by gravity, could load them. A constant flow of bulk transports, ground-effect surface freighters, came by special access routes to the port, unloaded their cargoes of foodstuff into the silos, and turned back again, bound for whatever harvest was presently going on.

The bogus barge carrying the *Falcon* settled to its appointed berth among hundreds of others on the field. They touched down, and the computers stopped their chatter. Han Solo and Chewbacca locked down the console and left the cockpit. As they entered the forward compartment, Bollux looked up. "Do we disembark now, sirs?"

"Nope," Han answered. "Jessa said these people we're going to pick up will find us."

The Wookiee went to the main lock and activated it. The hatch rolled up, and the ramp eased down, but didn't admit light or air from Orron III's atmosphere; the camouflaging hull design covered most of the *Fal-*

con's super-structure, and a makeshift outer hatch had been installed just beyond the ramp's end.

The ramp had barely lowered when there was a clanging on the outer skin there. The Wookiee snorted warily, and Han's hand dipped and came up with his blaster. Chewbacca, seeing his partner was ready, hit the switch to open the outer hatch.

Standing just beyond was a man of incongruities. He wore the drab green coveralls of a port worker and had a tool belt slung at his waist. Yet he radiated a different aura, nothing like that of a contract tech. He was native to a sun-plentiful world, that much was apparent, for his skin was so dark that its black approached indigo. He was half a head taller than Han, with broad shoulders that strained the seams of his issue coveralls, and a body that spoke of waiting, abundant power. His tightly curled black hair and sweeping beard were shot through with streaks of gray and white. For all the size and weight of dignity of him, he had a lively glint of humor in his black eyes.

"I'm Rekkon," he declared at once. He had a direct gaze, and although his tone was moderate, it resonated in the air, its quality deep and full. He replaced at his belt the heavy spanner he'd used to rap on the hatch. "Is Captain Solo here?"

Chewbacca gestured to his partner, who had just come further down the ramp. The Wookiee hooted in his own language. Rekkon laughed and—to their astonishment—roared back a polite response in Wookiee. Few enough humans even understood the giant humanoids' tongue; fewer still had the range and force of voice to speak it. Chewbacca boomed his delight in an earsplitting yowl and patted Rekkon's shoulder, beaming down at him.

"Now that you're all through with the community sing," Han interrupted, stripping off his flying gloves, "I'm Han Solo. When's liftoff?"

Rekkon appraised him frankly, but there was still that jovial light to his face. "I'd like it to be as soon as possible, as I'm sure you would, Captain Solo. But we must make one brief trip to the Center, to cull the data I need and pick up the other members of my group."

Han looked back to the head of the ramp, where Bollux waited, and gestured to him. "Let's go, Rusty. You're back in business."

Bollux, his chest plates closed once again, clanked down the ramp, his stride as stiff as ever. He'd explained during the trip that his odd manner of walking came from the fact that he'd been fitted with a heavy-duty suspension system at one point in his long career.

Rekkon was holding out two cards for Han and Chewbacca, bright red squares with white identification codes stamped on them. "Temporary IDs," he explained. "If anyone asks, you're on short-term labor contracts as tech assistants fifth class."

"Us?" Han sputtered. "We're not going anywhere, pal. You take the 'droid, get your gang and whatever else, and you come back. We'll keep the home fires burning."

Rekkon's grin was dazzling. "But what will you two do when the decontamination crew arrives? They'll be irradiating the entire barge, and your ship with it, to make sure no parasites feed on the shipment. Of course, you could switch on your deflector shields, but that would surely be noticed by port sensors." The two partners glanced at each other dubiously. It was true that a decontam-treatment would be normal procedure, and that a man and a Wookiee hanging around the landing area while the team did its work would make somebody curious.

"And there is another matter," Rekkon continued. "The Waiver status for your ship, and its doctored identification codes; I shall be taking care of those, too. Since you and your first mate have a vested interest in that, I had thought you might wish to accompany me."

Han's mouth began watering at the thought of the Waiver, but he always got the sweats in the halls of power, and that Authority Data Center was precisely that. His inbuilt caution came forward. "Why do you want us on this side trip? What is it you're not telling?"

"You're right, there are other reasons," Rekkon answered, "but I do think it best, for you as well as for me, if you come. I would be much in your debt."

Han stared at the tall black man, thinking about the Waiver and the inevitable decontam-team. "Chewie, get me a tool bag." He unfastened his blaster belt, knowing he couldn't be seen armed in an area of tight security. Chewbacca returned with the bag and his bowcaster. Both dropped their weapons into the tool bag, and the Wookiee slung it over his shoulder.

With Bollux trailing after, they walked through the outer hatch, locked it closed, and followed Rekkon across the maintenance gantry. The barge's hull stretched far below and to either side. A utility skimmer with a work platform and enclosed cab was hovering on the other side of the gantry. The living beings climbed into the cab, Rekkon getting behind the controls and Han crowding next to him, while Chewbacca filled the rear seat. Bollux settled himself on the work platform, securing himself with his servo-grip. The skimmer swung away from the barge.

"How'd you find us so fast?" Han wanted to know.

"I received word of what markings your craft would have, and its estimated time of arrival. I came as soon as the data systems registered your approach. I've been waiting here for some time, with forged field-access authorization. I presume this 'droid is my computer-probe?"

"Sort of," Han answered as Rekkon upped the skimmer's speed to the legal limit, guiding it between rows of berthed barges. "There's another unit built into his chest; that's your baby."

The port was surrounded on every side by ripening grain, showing the ripples of the gentle winds of Orron III. While he glanced about, Han asked, "What're you looking for in Authority computers, Rekkon?"

The man studied him for a moment, then turned back to the controls as he pulled onto a service road. Except for the immediate area of the barges, Han knew the skimmer would have to adhere to authorized routes, and would be intercepted if it flew too high, too fast, or cross-country. Off in the distance, gargantuan robot agricultural machines moved through the crops, capable of planting, cultivating, or harvesting vast tracts of land in a single day.

Rekkon adjusted the polarization of the skimmer's windshield and windows. He didn't make it reflective, or opaque to outside observation, which might have been conspicuous, but darkened it against the sun. The cab's interior dimmed, and Han felt as if he were in one of Sabodor's pet environment globes. As they sped along the service road, cutting between seas of bending grain, Rekkon asked, "Do you know what my mission here has been?"

"Jessa said it was up to you whether or not to tell us. I nearly passed up the bargain because of that, but I figured there must be a fair piece of cash involved for this kind of risk."

Rekkon shook his head. "Wrong, Captain Solo. It's a search for missing persons. The group I organized is made up of individuals who've lost friends or relatives under unexplained circumstances. Same thing's begun to happen with suspicious regularity within the Corporate Sector. I found that a number of others were abroad, as I was, seeking their lost ones. I'd detected a pattern, and so I gathered about me a small group of companions. We infiltrated the Data Center in order to carry out our search, with Jessa's help."

Han tapped his finger on the window, thinking. This explained Jessa's commitment to Rekkon and his group, her determination to see that he got all the required assistance. Doc's daughter obviously hoped that Rekkon and his bunch, in locating their own lost ones, would turn up her father.

"We've been here for nearly one Standard month," Rekkon continued, "and it's taken me most of that time to find windows of access into their systems, even though I'm rated as a contract computer tech supervisor first class. Their security is diligent, but not terribly imaginative."

Han shifted around on his seat to look at the other. "So what's the secret?"

"I won't say just yet; I'd rather be sure and have absolute proof. There is a final correlation of data for which I need a probe; the terminals to which I have access at the Center have governors and security limiters built into them. I lack the resources and parts and time to construct my own device. But I knew Jessa's excellent techs could provide what I needed and thereby decrease the risk of detection."

"Which reminds me, Rekkon. You haven't told us that other very good reason why we should come with you to the Center."

Rekkon looked pained. "You're persistent, Captain. I selected my companions carefully; each of them was close to a lost one, yet—"

Han sat up. "But you've got a traitor in there somewhere." Rekkon stared hard at the pilot. "It wasn't just a guess. Jessa's operation got hit while I was there; an Authority corvette dropped a spread of fighters on us. The chances of them just stumbling onto us, out of all the star systems in the Corporate Sector, are so small they're not even worth talking about. That left a spy, but not one who was there at the time, or the Espos wouldn't have been scouting, they'd have come in force. They must've been checking out a number of solar systems." He leaned back, self-satisfied. He was proud of his chain of logic.

Rekkon's face was a mask cut from jet. "Jessa gave us a contingency list of places where we might be able to contact her if our lines of communication were broken. Plainly, that solar system was one of them."

That surprised Han. Jessa would never ordinarily have trusted anyone with that sort of information. She must be investing all hope of finding her father with Rekkon. "Okay, so you've got somebody who's on two payrolls. Any idea who?"

"None, except that it cannot be either of the two members of my group who have already perished. I believe they discovered who the traitor was. There were indications in the final com-link conversation I had with one of them before she died. And so, of course, I've told no one of your arrival, and came to meet you myself. I wanted your help, to make sure none of them can give the alarm before we depart. I have called each of them to my office, without telling them the others would be there."

Han disliked the idea of going to the Center even more now, but saw it was vital that Rekkon have help, vital to the survival of Han Solo. If the traitor managed to turn in an alarm, chances were that the *Falcon* would never raise ship again. He made a mental note to bill Jessa and whoever else he could for additional services rendered. He angled around in his seat again. "Who're the other people you recruited for Amateur Night?"

Driving with only part of his attention, Rekkon responded, "My second-in-command is Torm, whose cover role is contract laborer. His family controlled large ranges on Kail, independent landowners under the Authority. There was some sort of dispute over land-use rights and stock prices. Several family members vanished when they wouldn't yield to pressure."

"Who else?"

"Atuarre. She is a female of the Trianii, a feline race. The Trianii had settled a planet on the fringes of Authority space generations before the Corporate Sector was chartered. When the Authority finally annexed the Trianii colony world recently, they met with resistance. Atuarre's mate disappeared and her cub was taken from her and placed in Authority custody. They must have used some sort of interrogation procedure on the cub, Pakka, for when Atuarre finally managed to rescue him, he could no longer speak. The Authority is no respecter of ages or conventions, you see. Atuarre and Pakka eventually made contact with me; her cover here on Orron III is that of apprentice agronomist."

The service road, winding through the fields, had met a main artery leading toward the Center. The place was a small city unto itself, handling record keeping, computations, and data flow and retrieval for much of the Corporate Sector. It radiated from an operations complex that rose like a glittering confection from the rolling farmland.

Rekkon, lips pursed in thought, wasn't finished. "The last member of our group is Engret, who is scarcely more than a boy, but has a good heart and a kindly temperament. His sister was an outspoken legal scholar, and she too dropped from sight." He was silent for a moment. "There are others abroad searching for their lost ones, and many more, I'm certain, who've been frightened into silence. But perhaps we shall be able to help them, too."

Han half snickered. "No way, Rekkon. I'm just here as part of a trade-off. Save the old school fight songs until I'm clear, got it?"

Rekkon's face was sculpted in amusement. "You only do this sort of thing so that you can become a wealthy man?" He eyed Han up and down and went back to his driving, but added, "A callous exterior isn't an uncommon way of protecting ideals, Captain; it hides the idealists from the derision of fools and cowards. But it also immobilizes them, so that, in trying to preserve their ideals, one risks losing them."

What this big, bluff, amiable man had just said carried so much of hit and of miss, insult and compliment, that Han didn't take time to unravel it. "I'm a guy with a hot ship and places to go, Rekkon, so don't let yourself get carried away with the philosophy."

They entered the Center, maneuvering along wide streets between rearing buildings housing the various offices and storage banks, personnel dormitories and recreational areas, shops and commissaries. The traffic was thick—robo-hacks, ground-effect cargo lifters, skimmers, Espo cruisers, and innumerable mechanicals.

Making a final turn, Rekkon entered a subterranean garage and descended more than ten levels. Nosing the skimmer into a vacant spot, he cut the engine and stepped out. Han and Chewbacca followed as Bollux clambered down. The Wookiee and his partner affixed their badges to their chests and vests, respectively. Rekkon slipped out of his coveralls and tool belt and stuffed both into an equipment locker on the skimmer's side. That left him attired in long, flowing robes of bright, geometric patterns. His supervisor's badge was prominent on his broad chest. His feet were shod in comfortable-looking sandals. Han asked him how he'd gotten the skimmer and other equipment.

"Not difficult, once I'd made a partial penetration of the computer systems. A false job-request form, an altered vehicle-allocation slip—those things were elementary."

Chewbacca took up the tool bag again. Bollux, who hadn't had the chance before, now drew himself up before Rekkon. "Jessa has instructed me to place myself and my autonomous computer module completely at your service."

"Thank you—Bollux, isn't it? Your aid will be critical to us." At this, the old 'droid seemed to straighten with pride. Han saw that Rekkon had found the way to Bollux's heart, or rather, to his behavioral circuitry matrix.

The Authority had spared no expense on this Center, and so, rather than to an elevator or shuttle car, it was to a lift chute that Rekkon led them. They stepped into its confluence and, seemingly standing on air, were wafted upward by the chute's field. Two techs drifted into the lift chute on the next level, and conversation among Han's group stopped. The Wookiee, the two men, and the 'droid continued to ascend, with others entering or leaving the field, for another minute and more, rising past garage and service levels, the lower bureacratic offices, and at last through the levels where data processing and retrieval operations of one kind and another took place. Most passengers in the chute wore computer techs' tunics. Occasionally, one would exchange a greeting with Rekkon. Han gathered, from the lack of curiosity he and his companions drew, that it wasn't unusual for a supervisor to have tech assistants and 'droids in tow.

Rekkon eventually tilted himself, to drift into the disembarkation-flow. Han, Chewbacca, and Bollux followed. They found themselves standing in a large gallery. Here, two floors had been combined, the upper one opening onto a balcony that ran around the gallery's midsection, looking down on the banks of lift and drop chutes.

Rekkon led on, down a hallway of darkly reflective walls, floor, and ceiling. Han caught sight of himself in the tinted mirror of the walls and wondered how he had ever wound up a reckless-eyed predator, contaminating these antiseptic inner domains of the juggernaut Authority. What he did know was that he would much rather have been hotting the *Falcon* along between the stars, unencumbered.

Rekkon stopped at a door and covered its lock face with his palm, then stepped through as the door swished open. The others followed him into a spacious, high-ceilinged chamber, three walls of which were lined with a complex array of computer terminals, systems monitors, access gear, and related equipment. The fourth wall, opposite the door, a single sheet of transparisteel, gave a commanding view of the bountiful fields of Orron III from one hundred meters up. Han went over and took a bearing on the spaceport across the gentle rise and fall of the land. Chewbacca, seating himself by the door on a bench that ran the length of the wall there, laid the tool bag down between his long, hairy feet. He watched the chatter and wink of sophisticated technology with only mild curiosity showing on his face.

Rekkon turned to Bollux. "Now, may I see what it is that you've brought me?"

Han clucked to himself softly, amazed that anyone should be so palsy-walsy with a mere 'droid.

Bollux's plastron opened as the stubby 'droid pulled his long arms back out of the way. The computer-probe's photoreceptor came on. "Hi!" he perked. "I'm Blue Max."

"You certainly are," Rekkon answered in his full, amused bass. "If your friend here will release you, we'll have a look at you, Max."

Bollux said an unhurried, "Of course, sir." There were minute clicks from his chest, the withdrawal of connector jacks and retaining pins. Rekkon drew the computer forth without trouble. Max was smaller than a voice-writer; he looked unimposing in Rekkon's big hands.

Rekkon's laughter rang. "If you were much smaller, Blue Max, I'd have to throw you back!"

"What's that mean?" Max asked dubiously.

Rekkon crossed to one of several worktables. "Nothing. A joke, Max." The table, a thick slab resting on a single service pillar, was studded with outlets, connectors, and complex instrumentation. Along its front edge ran an extremely versatile keyboard.

"How would you like to do this, Max?" Rekkon asked. "I have background and programming data to feed you, information on systems-intrusion. Then I'll patch you into the main network."

"Can you feed it in Forb Basic?" Max piped in his high, childish voice, like an eager kid with a new challenge.

"That presents no difficulty; I see you have a five-tine input." Rekkon drew a five-tine plug and line from his table and connected it to Max's side. Then he took a data plaque from his robes and inserted it into an aperture in the table, punching up the proper sequence on the keyboard. Max's photoreceptor darkened as the little computer gave his complete attention to the input. Several screens in the room came to life, giving high-speed displays of the information Max was ingesting.

Rekkon joined Han Solo at the window-wall and handed him another plaque, one he'd taken from his worktable. "Here is the new ship's ID for your Waiver. Alter your other documentation accordingly, and you should have no further problem with mandatory-performance profiles within the Corporate Sector."

Han bounced the plaque once or twice on his palm, visualizing enough money to wade through with his pants rolled up, then tucked it away.

"The rest of this shouldn't take terribly long," Rekkon explained. "The others in my group are due to show up in short order, and I don't expect someone with Max's brainpower to find this task too difficult.

76

But I'm afraid there's nothing in the way of refreshment around here—an oversight of mine."

Han shrugged. "Rekkon, I didn't stop off to eat, drink, or observe quaint local ceremonies. If you really want to make me dizzy with delight, just wrap it up here as fast as you can." He glanced around the room, with its perplexing lights and racing equations. "Are you honestly a computer expert, or did you get the job on sheer charm?"

Rekkon, hands on lapels, gazed out the window. "I'm a scholar by trade and inclination, Captain. I've studied a good many schools of the mind and disciplines of the body, as well as an array of technologies. I've lost track of my degrees and credentials, but I'm more than qualified to run this entire Center, if that's of any importance. At one point I specialized in organic-inorganic thought interfaces. That notwithstanding, I came here with forged records, playing the part of a supervisor, because I wished to remain inconspicuous. My only desire is to locate my nephew, and the others."

"What makes you think they're here?"

"They're not. But I believe their whereabouts can be discovered here. And when Max over there has helped me do that, by sifting through the general information here, I shall know where I must go."

"You never did get around to mentioning your own lost one," Han reminded him, thinking that he was beginning to sound like Rekkon. The man was infectious.

Rekkon paced to the opposite wall, stopping near Chewbacca. Han came after him, watching the man lost in thought. Rekkon took a seat, and Han did the same. "I raised the boy as if he were my son; he was quite young when his parents died. Not long ago, I was hired as instructor at an Authority university on Kalla. It is a place for higher education, mostly for Authority scions, a school rooted in technical education, commerce, and administration, with minimal stress on the humanities. But there were still some vacancies for a few old crackpots like me, and the pay was more than adequate. As nephew of a university don, the boy was eligible for higher study, and that's where the trouble began. He saw just how oppressive the Authority is, stifling anything that even remotely endangers profit.

"My nephew began to speak out and to encourage others to do the same." Rekkon stroked his dense beard as he thought back on it. "I advised him against doing so, although I knew he was right, but he had the convictions of youth, and I had acquired the timidity of age. Many of the students who listened to the boy had parents highly placed in the Authority; his words could not go unnoticed. It was a painful time, for although I couldn't ask the boy to ignore his conscience, I feared for him. As an ignoble compromise, I decided to resign my post. But before I could do so, my nephew simply disappeared.

"I went to the Security Police, of course. They made an appearance of concern, but it was clear that they had no intention of exerting themselves. I began making inquiries of my own and heard accounts of other disappearances among those who'd inconvenienced the Authority. I'm accustomed to looking for patterns; one wasn't long in emerging.

"Picking carefully—very carefully, I assure you, Captain!—I gathered a close group of those who'd lost someone, and we began a careful penetration of this Center. Word had come to me of the disappearance of Jessa's father, Doc, as he's called. I approached her, and she agreed to help us."

"All of which leaves us sitting here," Han interrupted, "but why here?"

Rekkon had noticed that the race of characters and ciphers across lighted screens had stopped. Rising to return to Max, he answered. "The disappearances are related. The Authority is attempting to remove those individuals who are most conspicuously against it; it has decided to interpret any natural, sentient individualism as an organized threat. I think the Authority has collected its opponents at some central location that—"

"Let me get this straight," Han broke in. "You think the Authority's gone into the wholesale kidnapping business? Rekkon, you've been staring at the lights and dials too long."

The man didn't look offended. "I doubt that the fact is generally known, even among Authority officials. Who can say how it happened? Some obscure official draws up a contingency proposal; an idle superior takes it seriously. A motivational study crosses the right desk perhaps, or a cost-benefit analysis becomes the pet project of a highly placed exec. But the germ of it was in the Authority all along—power and paranoia. Where no real opposition existed, suspicion supplied one."

As he spoke, he paced back to the worktable, unplugging Max. "That stuff was really interesting," the little computer bubbled.

"Please show a little less enthusiasm," Rekkon entreated, taking Max up from the table. "You give me the feeling I'm contributing to the delinquency of a minor." The computer's photoreceptor zeroed in on him as he continued. "Do you understand everything I've shown you?"

"You bet! Just give me a chance, and I'll prove it."

"I shall. The main event's coming up." Rekkon took Max over to one of the terminals and set him down by it. "You have a standard access adapter?" In reply, a small lid in the computer's side flipped down, and Max extended a short metal appendage. "Good, very good." Rekkon moved Max closer to the terminal. Max inserted his adapter into the disklike receptor there. The receptor and the calibrated dial around it circled around and back as Max accustomed himself to the fine points of the linkup.

"Please begin as soon as you're ready," Rekkon bade Max, and took a seat again between Han and Chewbacca. "He'll have to sift through an enormous amount of data," he told the two partners, "even though he can use the system itself to help him at his work. There are numerous security blocks; it will take even Blue Max awhile to find the right windows."

The Wookiee growled. Both humans understood the expression of Chewbacca's doubt that the information Rekkon wanted would actually be found in the network.

"The location as such won't be there, Chewbacca," Rekkon responded. "What Max will have to do is find it indirectly, just as you must sometimes turn your eyes away to locate a dim star, finding it out of the corner of your eye. Max will analyze logistical records, supply and patrol ship routings, communications flow patterns and navigational logs, plus a number of other things. We'll know where Authority ships have been stopping, and where coded traffic has been heaviest, and how many employees are on payrolls at various installations, and what their job categories are. In time, we'll find out where the Authority is keeping the members of what it has come to believe is a far-flung plot against it."

Rekkon got up again to pace the room briskly, clapping his hands with sounds like solid-projectile rifle shots. "These fools, these execs and their underlings, with their enemies' lists and Espo informers, they're creating just the sort of climate to make their worst fears come real. The prophecy fulfills itself; if we weren't talking about life and death here, it would make a grand joke!"

Han was reclining against the wall, watching Rekkon with a cynical smile. Had the scholar actually thought that people were any different from the Authority execs? Well, anybody who let his guard drop or wasted his time on ideals was in for just the same sort of rude shock Rekkon had gotten, Han thought. And that was why Han Solo had gone and would always go free among the stars.

He yawned elaborately. "Sure, Rekkon, the Authority better watch out. After all, what's it got going for it except a whole Sector's worth of ships, money, manpower, weapons, and equipment? What chance does it have against righteous thoughts and clean hands?"

Rekkon turned his hearty smile on Han. "But look at yourself, Captain. Jessa's communication mentioned a little about you. Just by living your life the way you chose, you've already committed deadly offenses against the Corporate Sector Authority. Oh, I don't look for you to wave a banner of freedom or to mouth platitudes. But if you think the Authority's the winning side, why aren't you playing its game? The Authority won't meet with disaster because it abuses naive schoolboys and idealistic old scholars. But as it increasingly hampers intractable, hardheaded individualists such as yourself, it will find its real opposition."

Han sighed. "Rekkon, you'd better take it easy; you've got me and Chewie confused with somebody else. We're just driving the bus. We're not the Jedi Knights, or Freedom's Sons."

What Rekkon's rejoinder would have been became academic. The door-lock buzzed just then, and a man's voice at the intercom demanded: "Rekkon! Open this door!"

With a cold feeling in his stomach, Han caught the blaster Chewbacca tossed to him as the Wookiee leveled his bowcaster at the door.

VI

REKKON interposed himself between Han and Chewbacca and the door. "Kindly put your weapons up, Captain. That is Torm, one of my group. Even if it weren't, would it not have been wiser to find out what was happening before preparing to shoot?"

Han made a sour face. "I happen to *like* to shoot first, Rekkon. As opposed to shooting second." But he lowered his weapon, and Chewbacca did the same with the bowcaster. Rekkon worked the door controls.

The panel snapped up, revealing a man of about

Han's height, but bulkier through the torso, with brawny arms and wide, blunt hands. His face was fine-featured, with high cheekbones and alert, roving eyes of a liquid blue. His hair was a long shock of bright red. His darting eyes found Han and Chewbacca first, as his right hand made a reflexive spasm toward the thigh pouch of his coveralls. But he arrested the motion, turning it into the rubbing of palm against trouser leg on seeing Rekkon. Han didn't blame the man for being skittish at this point, with several of his teammates already dead.

The man's mind worked quickly. "We're leaving?" he was asking, even as he stepped through the door.

"Presently," Rekkon replied, gesturing over to where Blue Max sat linked to the data system. "We'll soon have the data we require. Captain Solo there and his first mate, Chewbacca, will be transporting us off-world when we're ready. Gentlemen, may I present Torm, one of my companions."

Torm, his poise recovered now, inclined his head to the two, then went over to inspect Blue Max. Han followed; someone in this band might be an informer, and he wanted to acquaint himself with each one of them, to do all he could to safeguard himself and his ship.

"Not very impressive, is it?" Torm asked, staring down at Max.

"Not too," Han answered fake-pleasantly.

A nod from Torm. "You think Rekkon'll find what he's looking for?" Han asked. "I mean, this long shot's your only hope of finding your folks, right? Or shouldn't I ask?"

Torm fastened a frank gaze on him. "It *is* a personal matter, Captain. But since your own safety is at stake, I suppose you're within your rights. Yes, if I can't locate my father and brother in this way, I'll have no idea how to proceed. We've fixed all our hopes on Rekkon's theory." For a moment he glanced over to Rekkon, who was showing Chewbacca features of the room's equipment. "I didn't throw in with him lightly, but when I saw that the Authority was dragging its feet in its investigations, and my own inquiries led me to him, I knew I must commit myself to follow Rekkon's belief."

Torm's voice had drifted as his thoughts had. Now he came back to himself. "It's most unselfish, very admirable of you, Captain Solo, to take on this mission. Not many men would willingly risk—"

"Jet back; you got it all wrong," Han interrupted. "I'm here 'cause I struck a deal, Torm. I'm strictly a businessman. I fly for money and I look out for number one, clear?"

Torm reappraised him. "Quite. Thank you for clarifying that, Captain. I stand corrected."

The door was sounding again. This time, Rekkon admitted two of his co-conspirators. They were Trianii, members of a humanoid species of feline. One was an adult female, trim and supple, who stood just about the height of Han's chin. Her eyes were very large, yellow, with vertical slits of green iris. Her pelt, a varied, striped pattern along her back and sides, lightened to a soft, creamy color on face, throat, and torso front. It tufted out to a thick mane around her head, neck, and shoulders. Behind her curled and swayed a meter of restive tail, mixing the colors of her pelt. She wore the only clothing her species required, a belt at her hips to support loops and pouches for her tools, instruments, and other items. Rekkon introduced this being as Atuarre.

With Atuarre was her cub, Pakka. He was a miniature copy of his mother, standing half her height, but his coloring was darker, and he wasn't as slender or as graceful. He still had some of the fuzzier fur and baby fat of cubhood, but his wide eyes seemed to hold an adult's wisdom and sorrow. Though his mother spoke, Pakka said nothing. Then Han recalled Rekkon's saying the cub had been a mute since enduring Authority custody. Like his parent, Pakka wore a belt and pouches.

Atuarre pointed a slim, clawed finger at Han and Chewbacca. "What are they doing here?"

"They're here to aid our escape," Rekkon explained. "They brought the computer element I needed to extract the final data. The only one yet to arrive is Engret; I couldn't contact him, but left a message on his recorder with the code word for him to contact me."

Atuarre seemed agitated. "Engret didn't make his check-call and didn't answer his com, so I stopped by his billet on the way here. I'm sure his quarters are under surveillance; we Trianii do not mistake such things. Rekkon, I believe Engret's been killed, or taken."

The leader of the small band sat down. For a moment Han saw the strength and determination leave Rekkon's features. Then it was back, that special vitality. "I suspected that was the case," he admitted. "Engret would not forgo contact for days, no matter what. I trust your instincts in this completely, Atuarre. We must presume him to have been eliminated."

He had said this with absolute finality. This wasn't the first time he had come up against an unexplained disappearance. Han shook his head; on one side was the near-absolute power of the Authority, and on the other, nothing more substantial than friendship, than family ties. Han Solo, loner and realist, considered it a gross mismatch.

"How do we know he's what he says he is?" Atuarre was demanding, pointing to Han.

Rekkon looked up. "Captain Solo and his first mate, Chewbacca, come to us by way of Jessa. I presume we all trust her aid and counsel? Good. We leave as soon as possible; I'm afraid there'll be no time for luggage or arrangements. Or com-calls, for any of us."

Atuarre took her cub's paw-hand as Pakka studied Han and Chewbacca silently. "When do we go?"

Rekkon went back to Max, to find out just that. Just then the computer module's photoreceptor came back on. "Got it!" he chirped. A translucent data plaque emerged from the slot at the terminal's side.

Rekkon seized it eagerly. "Fine. Now we must match it against the Authority's installations charts—"

"But that's not all," Max blurted.

Rekkon's dense brows knit. "What more, Blue Max?"

"While I was in the system, I monitored it, you know, to get the feel. This intrusion is fun! Anyway, there's a Security alert on in the building. I think it's directed at this level. The Espos are moving into position."

Atuarre hissed and pulled her cub closer. Torm's face seemed impassive at first, but Han noticed a tic of anxiety along his jaw. Rekkon tucked the data plaque into his robes, and from them drew a big disrupter pistol. Han was already buckling on his gunbelt, as Chewbacca settled his ammo bandolier over his shoulder and threw the empty tool bag aside.

"Next time I fall for one of these tempting offers," Han instructed his partner, "sit on me till the urge passes."

Chewbacca growled that he definitely would.

Torm had taken a handgun from his thigh pocket, and Atuarre had produced another from one of her belt pouches. Even the cub, Pakka, was armed; he pulled a toylike pistol from his belt.

"Max," Rekkon said, "are you still in the network?" Max indicated he was. "Good. Now, look at deployment plans for alerts in this Center. At what corridors, junctions, and levels will the Espos be stationed?"

"I can't tell you that," Max answered, "but I could clear a way through them, if that's what you want."

That grabbed Han's attention. "What'd that little fusebox say?"

The computer-probe elaborated. "The Security Policemen are all supposed to respond to alarms, it says here, and redeploy to cover any new trouble spots. I could just make enough alarms in other places and draw them away in different directions."

"That may not get them all out of the way," Han pointed out, "but it could sure thin out the opposition. Do it, Maxie." Another thought struck him. "Wait a second. Can you fake alarms anywhere else?"

Max's voice burst with pride. "Anywhere on Orron III, Captain. This network's got so much capacity that they've hooked just about everything into it. Good cost reduction, but bad security, right, Captain?"

"No foolin'. Yeah, give it everything you've got: fires in the power plants, riots in the barracks, indecent exposure in the cafeteria, whatever appeals to you, all over the planet." He was thinking that if there *were* a picket ship in orbit, she might also be kept busy by a rash of false alarms.

Bollux, who had remained silent during all this commotion, now came to the terminal and prepared to take Max back the moment the computer's work was done. Rekkon stood with him.

"There're two ways out of here that might be open," Max announced, and flashed the positions on the screen. The two paths, picked out on the level's layout, both led back to the gallery where the lift and drop chute banks were located. One route was on their floor, the other on the floor above.

Security alarms began clanging and warbling in the corridors. The room's equipment blazed with ripples of light as every circuit reacted to Max's prompting. Then, suddenly, the room became dim, except for light from the window-wall. The Center's automatics had shut down main power sources in response to the supposed emergency. Alarms continued to sound, running on reserves.

"Illumination in the corridors will be very low, on standby power," Rekkon told the others as they gathered by the door. "We may be able to slip by." He carefully set Blue Max back into his emplacement. As his plastron swung shut, Bollux, followed by Rekkon, joined the rest of them at the door.

"If I may suggest," said the 'droid, "I would, perhaps, attract less suspicion than any other individual here. I could walk well in advance of you others, in case there are Security Policemen present."

"That makes sense," Atuarre said. "Espos won't waste time and power shooting a 'droid. They'll halt him, though, and that will warn us off from any traps."

The door slid up, and Bollux started off down the corridor, preceded by the noise of his stiff suspension.

The others followed after—Rekkon and Han in the lead, with Torm behind. Atuarre and Pakka came next, and Chewbacca brought up the rear, his bowcaster cocked and ready. The Wookiee was watching the conspirators as well as rear-guarding. With the possibility of a traitor in the group, he and Han trusted no one, not even Rekkon. The first wrong move on the part of any of them would be the Wookiee's signal to shoot.

They came to a turn. Bollux went around first, but as the others approached it, they heard:

"Halt! You, 'droid, get over here!"

Han, peeking cautiously around the corner, spied a contingent of heavily armed Espos clustered around Bollux. He picked up bits of the conversation, mostly questions about whether the 'droid had seen anyone else. Bollux put up a front of supreme ignorance and lethargic circuitry. Beyond the gathered Espos, the corridor opened onto the chute gallery, but it might just as well have been on the other side of the Corporate Sector.

"It's no good this way," Han said.

"Then it's the more desperate route for us," Rekkon replied. "Follow me." They went back the way they had come, at a trot. As they rounded the next corridor, the footfalls of the Espo detachment drifted to them. They hadn't gone far when they heard another squad approaching from the opposite direction.

"Nearest stairwell," Han instructed Rekkon, who led them a few meters more, then ducked through a door. "Keep it as quiet as you can," Han whispered in the semidarkness of the emergency-lighted stairwell. "Up one floor, and we'll make our way to the balcony overlooking the chutes." Of course, Chewbacca, for all his bulk, moved quietly, as did the sinuous Atuarre and her cub. Rekkon, too, seemed used to running with stealthy efficiency. That left only Han and Torm to guard their steps, both laboring to keep the noise of their movements to a minimum.

When they reached the second floor of that level, they found it empty. Blue Max's flurry of crazy alerts had drawn the security forces away from their contingency posts. The fugitives raced along the corridors as through a hall of mirrors, keeping close to the walls.

They came to the balcony overlooking the gallery. Crouching low, they edged up to its railing. Han risked a quick peek over the top, then drew his head down again. "They're setting up a crew-served blaster down by the chutes," he told them. "There're three Espos working it. Chewie and I will fix that up; the rest of you get set to jump. Chewie?"

The Wookiee rumbled softly, his finger tightening on the bowcaster. He moved off, staying low, along the railing. Han leaned close to Rekkon's ear and whispered, "Do us a favor and watch things here; we can only look one way at a time." He scuttled off in the opposite direction from his partner. With Rekkon armed and watchful, Han doubted that any turncoat would show his hand now.

He paralleled the railing, rounding its corner, down to the far wall. Peering over the rail, he saw the Wookiee's big blue eyes edging up over the opposite railing. Halfway between them and several meters below, the gun crew was making final adjustments on the heavy blaster and its tripod mount. In a moment they would be ready to activate the weapon's deflector shield; going after them would then become an almost hopeless venture, and the drop chutes would be inaccessible. Apprehension would be a matter of time. One of the Espos was bending even now to throw on the shield.

Han stood, drew, fired. The man who had been about to activate the shield slumped, clasping a burned leg. But one of the others, with no regard for niceties like fire-discipline, spun and sprayed a steady stream of destructive energy from a short riot gun. The riot gun's fire blasted material from the walls and railing; the Espo slewed the weapon around carelessly, searching for his target.

Han was forced to duck back out of the way as the rain of energy lashed through the air, striking walls, ceiling, and most things in between. That innocent by-standers might've been hurt didn't seem to have entered into the Espo's calculations.

But the Espo gave a cry and fell, his finger easing off the trigger, accompanied by the metallic twang of Chewbacca's bowcaster. Han looked over the rail again and saw the second man slumped over the first, brought down by one of the short quarrels from the Wookiee's weapon. Now Chewbacca stood, jacking the foregrip of his bowcaster down to recock it and strip another round off its magazine.

The third gun crewman kicked the bodies of his fellows out of the way while firing wildly with his pistol and yelling for help. Han shot him just as the Espo's hands were closing on the heavy blaster's grips. Chewbacca was already over the balcony railing. Han, straddling the railing on his side, called, "Rekkon, get 'em moving!" He pushed himself off.

He missed his footing and fell to all fours, then raced to help his partner throw assorted Espos off the blaster cannon. Torm leaped down, landing lightly for all his weight, and Atuarre came after him, all grace and form. Her cub launched himself off the rail, gathered his limbs and tail in for a somersault, and landed next to her. Atuarre slapped him on his way, as if to say this was no place to show off, even for an acrobatic Trianii.

Last to come was Rekkon, moving skillfully, as if this were something he did all the time. Han wondered for a half-second about this versatile university don who never seemed to lose track of the problems at hand. In sending all the others ahead, Rekkon made sure no potential spy remained behind, to be tempted by an unguarded back.

Torm stopped short of the drop chutes, luckily for him. "The fields have been shut off!" he shouted. Rekkon and Atuarre were with him in a moment, fumbling at the emergency panel beside the chute opening. Rekkon's sturdy fingers closed around the panel's grille, and he yanked it away without apparent effort.

Calls and a general hubbub could be heard in the upper corridors. Han squirmed himself down behind the blaster cannon, setting his feet on the pegs of its tripod, and switched on the deflector shield. "Heads up!" he warned his companions. "The party's starting!"

A squad of Espos, wearing combat armor and carrying rifles and riot guns, burst out onto the balcony above, fanning out along the rail, and started firing down. Their bolts splashed in polychrome waves from the cannon's shield. Torm, Rekkon, and the others, directly behind Han as they worked on the drop-chute panel, were protected, too, for now. Chewbacca stood behind his partner, firing his bowcaster whenever he had an opening. Soon his weapon was empty, and he pulled another magazine from his bandolier. He chose explosive quarrels and started firing again. The detonations filled the gallery with smoke and thunder.

Han had raised the cannon's snout to extreme elevation, and now he swept it across the railing. Heavy blaster charges flashed and crackled; parts of the railing and the balcony's edge exploded, melted, or burst into flames. Several Espos were hit, falling to the floor below, and the rest backed hastily out of the line of fire, darting out to snap off a volley when they could, in a constant, determined exchange of shots. The firefight and its echoes, heat, and smoke enveloped the gallery.

Han kept the Espos' heads down with long traverses of the cannon, letting go at the floor of the balcony, scoring the walls. The gallery heated up like a furnace from the energies unleashed. Red beams of annihilation bickered back and forth, and Han knew that the cannon's shield wouldn't hold out forever against constant fire from the riot guns and rifles.

A squad of armored figures appeared in the low corridor, the one leading directly onto the gallery. Han depressed the cannon's mouth and filled the lower hallway with raging destruction. These Espos drew back, too, but, like the others, stayed just out of range to risk firing whenever they could. Atuarre, Pakka, and Torm, drawing their guns, joined Han and Chew-bacca in returning fire, while Rekkon kept working at the chute.

"Rekkon, if you can't get that drop field working, that'll be all for us," Han hollered over his shoulder. A Security man leaned out from the balcony above and snapped off a shot. It rebounded from the gun's shield, but Han could tell from the residual heat the deflector let through that it was beginning to fail.

"It's no use," Rekkon decided as his strong, sensitive fingers probed the mechanisms. "We'll have to find another way out."

"This is a one-way street!" Han shouted without looking back. Chewbacca's angry, frustrated roars sounded above the din.

"Then *you* dive headfirst down the shaft!" Torm bellowed back. Han's rejoinder was lost in an electronic whooping that filled all their ears, catching at their hearts. It was a warning signal, standard throughout much of the galaxy.

"Hard radiation leak," Rekkon shouted. "That wasn't one of the alarms Max put in."

Not only that, Han thought, but it had only just begun to sound, and it was sounding right in the corridors off the gallery. A hard radiation exposure would leave little chance for any of them to live; they'd be receiving lethal dosages even as they listened. Han swore at himself for ever having gotten out of a nice, cushy racket like gunrunning sideways through mountains. He scrambled up. "Get ready. We're going to have to shoot our way through them, or else we all get signed off."

Over the alert sirens, Atuarre shrilled, "Wait—look!"

Han's blaster was out again, ready to target on what he presumed to be another Espo. But the figure tottering down the lower hall toward them was moving stiffly, its arms extended horizontally, holding some burden.

"Bollux!" cried Torm, and it was. The 'droid stiff-legged out into the stronger light of the gallery, holding a globular public-address speaker in either hand. Wires from them ran back to his open chest, patched in near Blue Max's emplacement. From the speakers beat the whooping radiation alarm.

They gathered around Bollux, yelling in Standard, Wookiee, Trianii, and one or two other tongues, but nobody could hear anybody else because of the alarms. Han was getting a headache that he was willing to ignore only because he was too overjoyed at being alive.

Then the alarms stopped. Bollux carefully lowered the P.A. speakers and patiently unplugged their cables from himself while the others clamored for an explanation.

"I'm gratified that my plan worked, sirs and ma'am; but I confess it was merely an extension of Max's false alarms," Bollux told them. "He learned about the radiation alarms while he was in the network. Under his guidance, I vandalized these two speakers from the corridor walls and adapted them. The corridors are empty now; the Espo armor is for combat, not radiation protection. They appear to have withdrawn hastily."

Han broke in, "Get Max over there by the drop chutes. If he can't get one running again, we're still gonna be old news." He tugged Bollux over that way.

"All the chutes cut out, right?" Blue Max piped up. "No sweat, Captain!"

"Just turn 'em on, huh?" Han pleaded, adding, "What's a runt like you know about sweat, anyway?"

Bollux's plastron swung wide as the 'droid approached the panel. But the adapter input was too high. So Chewbacca, who was closest, slung his bowcaster, took Max out of his emplacement, and held the computer up to the chute's control panel. Max's adapter extended itself and engaged the receptor. The metal tumblers twirled back, forth, back again. The panel lit up.

"It's working!" Rekkon exulted. "Quickly, follow me, before someone notices and has the thing shut down again." He made a hand motion to Han, so fast that no one else caught it, and the pilot knew he was to go last. Rekkon was still unsure of the loyalty of his people. He hopped into the drop chute and Atuarre followed after him. Then came Pakka, spinning, tumbling, and chasing his own tail playfully in the chute's field. Torm leaped after, gun in hand.

They could hear the tread of cleated boots in the corridor. With Blue Max still tucked under his arm, Chewbacca jumped into the drop chute, too. Han held back long enough to fire at the blaster cannon from its unshielded side. There was a bright eruption as its power pack began to overload. Han spun and dived headlong down the shaft, as Torm had invited him to do. Behind, he heard the explosion of the portable cannon.

They plunged down, in varying postures and attitudes, strung out behind Rekkon in a ragged line. Craning their heads upward, they waited nervously for the first blaster bolt to come raving down the chute, but none did. Han decided that the Espos had been delayed by the exploding cannon. He hoped it would take them awhile to figure out that the drop chute was on, but feared that any moment would bring the stomach-wrenching fall, once the field was shut down again, that would plunge him, Chewie—all of them—to their deaths.

They descended all the way to the garage levels. Rekkon left the chute at last, beckoning them to do the same. They found themselves standing in a large parking area as alarms sounded off in the distance. "I thought there would be a flyer of some sort here," Rekkon said sourly; "worse luck."

"We're not going back into that chute, and that's that," Han stated.

"There's a ground skimmer. Let's take it," Atuarre suggested. They piled in, with Han taking the controls and Rekkon next to him. Chewbacca sat back in the cargo bed with the others, keeping his back to his partner and his eyes on the others as he fit a new magazine into his bowcaster. Before the Wookiee

93

could take time to return Max to Bollux's chest, Han had thrown the skimmer into motion and shot away, barely making the turn onto the up-ramp, scarcely avoiding the wall.

He kept the control stem's steering grips pushed forward, giving the skimmer all the acceleration she could safely stand and a good deal more. The ramp went by in a wild corkscrewing of Formex, the walls whirling past the skimmer's front cowling at hair-raising speed. Rekkon saw at once the wisdom of yielding the controls to the younger man.

Han hoped that nobody had gotten around to sealing off the computer complex yet, and they hadn't. The security network was inundated with everything from reports of insurrection to drunk-and-disorderly calls from the executives' club, spread across the Center and the face of Orron III. The skimmer left the garage like a missile out of a launch tube. In his haste, Han had departed through a door clearly marked ENTRANCE. A traffic-monitoring scanner dutifully logged the skimmer's license number for a citation and mandatory court appearance.

The skimmer tore through the city, guided partly by Rekkon's instructions and partly by Han's instincts. Han left the city's edge behind in a blur, drilling a hole through the air down the fusion-formed road, as other traffic dodged and skidded hysterically away from him. He was glad he'd taken the time to orient himself on the spaceport while in Rekkon's office. Since its cab was open, the wind plucked and tugged hard at everyone on the skimmer, ruffling hair, fur, and clothing alike, making conversation impossible as the passengers braced however and wherever they could.

But rounding a turn in the last stretch approaching the spaceport, Han discovered that somebody somewhere in the bureaucracy had actually done a bit of thinking. The skimmer nearly crashed head-on into a roadblock, an Espo troop-hovervan parked across the roadway, its twin-mounted guns nosing for a target.

Han jerked the controls hard, kicking the foot auxiliaries, and sent his small vehicle sailing off the road's surface. The engine sang with effort; the low-built skimmer slammed down among the rippling grain and raced off through it erratically. The tall grain, an Arcon Multinode hybrid, was so high that it instantly swallowed them up, hiding them from the startled Espos. But Han zigzagged anyway, for luck, and sure enough, the Espos fired even though they had no clear target, most probably from sheer frustration. The troop-hovervan was a ground-effect vehicle, unable to climb above the field, Han knew. That meant that if his pursuers wanted to give chase, they'd have to eat a little cereal themselves.

He had to stand up, poking his head above the windscreen as he drove, in a mostly unsuccessful attempt to see where he was going. The skimmer sliced through thick rows of hybrid grain, sending a spray of mangled plants and chaff back over and around it. Han slitted his eyes and tried to peer through the hurricane of vegetable matter as best he could, which wasn't very well. In moments, all of the skimmer's grillwork and trim was decked with stalks of grain that had gotten lodged there, and the craft looked like a strange agricultural float.

Chewbacca, standing and exhorting, reached forward over his partner's shoulder and pointed. Han, asking no questions, changed course. He had to steer hard to slide past the hazard, a mountain of yellow metal, one of the enormous automated farm machines slowly and patiently working this part of Orron III's limitless fields.

Han broke out onto bare ground, reaped clean by the harvester. He conned the skimmer around in a wide arc, got his bearings on the spaceport and the ranked colossi of the berthed barges, and hotted off that way.

At that moment the Espo hovervan broke through, too, but farther down the field, away from the spaceport. Han couldn't take time to watch it; instead he tried to throw enough twists and dodges into his course to keep them out of the Espo gunner's sights. Heavy blaster salvos scored around the skimmer, starting small fires smoldering among the stubble of shorn stalks.

Han took the skimmer through a hairpin turn, trying to jump out of the line of fire, but the hovervan's twin-mounted guns scored closer and closer to starboard, making the shaven field erupt. He jammed the control stem back to port. But the Espo gunner, trying for a bracketing salvo, had outguessed him. The ground blew apart just beyond the skimmer's undercarriage.

The skimmer jarred violently, its nose plowing at the rich soil, crumpling, as the engine cowling was smashed and compressed. Smoke rolled from its engine compartment, and the little craft grounded, carving long scars in the crop-stubble.

Han, fighting to keep control, lost his grip on the control stem at the last moment, clipped his head on the windscreen, and was flung clear of the cab as it stopped short, ending up on his back. He watched the sky of Orron III, which appeared to be spinning, and wondered if his entire skeleton had actually been turned into confetti. That was just how he felt.

"Everybody off," he announced woozily; "baggage claim to your left."

The others tumbled off the wrecked skimmer. Han found himself being lifted as easily as a child; Rekkon's dark fists were hoisting him by his vest. He was pleased to find himself more or less whole. "Run for the spaceport fence!" Rekkon ordered the others. The whine of the Espo hovervan grew in the distance.

Han shook off the fall. The hovervan was closing quickly. Rekkon pulled him down into the shelter of the skimmer's nose and began working at the adjustments of his oversized disrupter pistol. Han drew his blaster. "Chewie, get 'em moving," he called.

The vociferous Wookiee, still lugging Blue Max in one arm, shoved or shouted the others into motion. Atuarre and Pakka sped away, the Trianii female half dragging her cub, half carrying him, with Torm not far behind. Even Bollux moved at top speed in long, jarring bounds made possible by his heavy-duty suspension system, disregarding the damage he might do his gyros and shock absorbers. Chewbacca came last, casting frequent glances over his shoulder. Before them rose another stand of grain, being reaped by another of the giant machines, and past that was the spaceport security fence.

Han felt a warm liquidity on his forehead, swiped at it, and saw blood on his fingers, courtesy of the skimmer's windscreen. Rekkon, having finished adjusting his disrupter, was waiting for the hovervan to come into range, which it was doing with frightening speed.

The hovervan driver, watching the figures running for the fence, failed to notice the two men hiding behind the disabled vehicle. When the Espo was close enough, Rekkon, forearms braced across the skimmer's nose, fired. He'd set his disrupter on overload, and now the powerful handgun emptied itself in a brief flood of ruinous energy. Han had to shield his face from it, thinking what a chance Rekkon was taking; the disrupter could just as easily have blown up in his hands, killing both men.

But the jet of disrupter fire splashed across the hovervan's cowling and windshield. The Espo craft slid side-on, spun once, and planed into the ground, plowing up a mound of soil before it.

Han, lowering his hands, saw that the barrel of Rekkon's pistol was white-hot, and the scholar's face was sweating and seared. Rekkon tossed aside the useless pistol. "You must've taught in some tough damn schools," was Han's only comment as he struggled to his feet, preparing to run again.

Rekkon, watching the overturned hovervan, didn't hear. Body-armored Espos were already stumbling from it, to continue the pursuit on foot. The twin-gun mount, twisted underneath the vehicle, was useless. Rekkon, backing away a step or two, said, "The moment has come for our departure, Captain Solo!"

Han pegged a couple of shots at the Espos. The range was long, but they still hit the dirt. Then he put his head down and pounded off behind Rekkon, wondering if the Espos could get into range before the fugitives made the fence and somehow got over, under, or through it. All things considered, the smart money appeared to be with the Espos, he conceded.

For long moments all he did was race after Rekkon's flying sandals and wait for a blaster bolt to fry his shoulder blades. Then he raised his head, gulping breath. The monstrous harvester was working its way back down the rows of grain, its gaping maw cutting down a swatch twenty meters wide, pouring the grain into a tandem load-carrier. Han and Rekkon cut wide around it, and Han scanned the terrain in front of him. He spotted figures thrashing through the stalks, but could make none of them out.

A shot kicked up dirt and flame off to the left, proof that the Espos were gaining. Han and Rekkon dodged right, to put the enormous agrirobot between themselves and their pursuers. Then they were shoving, running, tearing through a world of golden-red stalks, occasionally spying one of their companions in the distance.

Han dug his heels in, sliding to a stop. Rekkon, who'd come abreast of him, caught the movement and halted, too. Both of them panted hard, as Han demanded, "Where's Chewie?"

"Ahead of us, to the side; who can tell in this field?"

"He's not. He's the only one who'd be easy to spot, even here." Han straightened, his side aching. "That means he's back there!" He shagged back the way he'd come, ignoring Rekkon's cries.

When he broke into the open again, he saw at once what had happened. Chewbacca had realized the Espos stood a good chance of overtaking his companions before they could make it to the spaceport and get past the fence. Some major distraction had been needed to save all their lives, and so the Wookiee had paused to set one up.

As Han cried out for him to come back, Chewbacca, his bowcaster slung over his shoulder and Blue Max under his long arm, pulled himself up the side of the giant harvester as the machine went on its preprogrammed way. The harvester had already borne the Wookiee most of the way back toward the Espos. He finished climbing the last few feet, reaching the top of the agrirobot, where its control center was situated.

Chewbacca began tugging and heaving at the protective cover over the controls. It was a durable industrial design and resisted him. Han and Rekkon watched as Chewbacca seated himself for better leverage, then applied all his strength in a tremendous effort. The cover popped loose, and the Wookiee threw it aside. He began working furiously, uncoupling hookups and moving components around in order to make room for Blue Max. There was no way he could hear Han's hoarse shouts over the noise of the harvester, and the distance, and no way could the Wookiee see, from his position, the three Espos who had managed to catch hold of one of the maintenance ladders and clamber after him.

Han was too far away to shoot. The Espos swarmed quickly upward. The huge harvester gave a lurch, then went through a series of disturbed tremors as Blue Max usurped control of it and tried his touch. Just as the Espos, having worked their way to the top of the ladder, leveled their weapons at Chewbacca's spine, the harvester gave the most violent shudder of all.

One Espo nearly fell, and must have yelled, because the Wookiee's head snapped around just as the three crouched to keep from being dislodged. Chewbacca's bowcaster shot exploded against one man's chest, flinging him backward to roll off the harvester's side. But in turning and firing, Chewbacca had lost his own balance. The harvester went into a sharp turn, and the Wookiee had to make a desperate lunge to catch hold of a stanchion. He managed to do it but lost hold of his bowcaster.

"Chewie!" Han bawled, starting back, but Rekkon's big hand closed around his shoulder, holding him resolutely.

"You can't get to him now," the scholar shouted,

and that seemed certain. More Espos were closing in around the slow-moving harvester.

Chewbacca, unarmed, got his feet back under him and threw himself at the two remaining Espos before they could recover. He gathered one in a lethal hug, kicking the second, before either man could raise his weapon. But the second man somehow managed to cling to the Wookiee's leg, and held on for his life.

Blue Max now had the harvester under control, that much was clear. He pivoted the machine, attempting to swallow an entire squad of Espos. But, using the harvester's primitive guidance system, Max was unaware of the Wookiee's predicament. The pivot dislodged Chewbacca and the two Espos. They fell, limbs gyrating, and the Wookiee somehow managed to land on top. But it was still a long drop, and before the stunned humanoid could rise, he was buried under a pile of rifle-swinging Espos.

Han, struggling to get loose of Rekkon's grip, felt himself shaken until his teeth rattled. Rekkon implored, "There are dozens of them! You have no hope. Better to live, and stay free, to help the Wookiee later!"

Han spun, pulling his blaster. "Hands off. I mean it."

Rekkon saw by his eyes that he did indeed; Han would kill anyone who stood between himself and Chewbacca. The broad black hands fell away. Gun in hand, Han went off toward the mass of Espos.

He couldn't tell just how Rekkon hit him then. Han's whole spinal column seemed to light up, and a blinding paralysis descended on him. Perhaps it was a nerve-punch, or a blow to a spot selected for its hydrostatic shock value. In any case, Han dropped like an unstrung puppet.

The harvester, moving much more quickly now, circled back at the Espos. They fired on it, but the giant machine, an uncomplicated device, was difficult to stop with small-arms fire. Unimportant pieces of plating and cutter blade were shot away, but the harvester ground on. Several Espos, failing to move quickly enough in the thick grain, vanished into its cavernous mouth.

Max had finally seen Chewbacca's predicament and moved in to give the Wookiee an opportunity to jump back aboard. But Chewbacca, his arms and legs dangling limply, was now being rushed away by a squad of Espos. Max couldn't go after them for fear of injuring Chewbacca with the clumsy harvester. Moreover, the Espos' fire was becoming more concentrated. Blue Max wished desperately that Bollux were there to tell him what to do; the computer didn't feel that he'd been operative long enough to make decisions like this one. But with no other apparent option, Max recognized that he must go join the others. He headed the ponderous harvester around, cut out its speed governor, and gunned it for all it was worth.

Han only dimly felt Rekkon hoist him up on one shoulder; he could hardly focus his eyes. But as Max came past, Rekkon took a pair of wide steps, propelled himself into the air, and caught a foothold at the harvester's side. He pulled himself up a short ladder and deposited Han on a narrow catwalk. Somehow, Han managed to lift his head. He could make out, through the machine's rough ride and the distance, the knot of Espos bearing his friend away, a prisoner.

Han clawed at the metal under him, to throw himself off the machine, to go back. Rekkon was on him instantly, pinning his arms with a strength and an intensity that were frightening. "He's my friend!" Han grimaced, writhing.

Rekkon shook him once more, with more emphasis than violence. "Then *help your friend!*" urged the rich basso voice. "Face hard fact: you must save yourself to save him, and not throw both lives away!"

The giant, imprisoning strength retreated and Han was left enervated, knowing Rekkon was right. Holding the catwalk railing, he stopped staring at the indistinguishable specks of Chewbacca and the Espos.

"Ahh." He lowered his eyes disconsolately. "Chewie . . ."

VII

AS he overtook each of the escapees in turn, Max slowed the harvester just enough for them to board. First was Bollux, who had fallen behind the others despite his best efforts; he made a last bound with a deep *sproing* from his suspension, found a servo-grip hold, and drew himself aboard. Then came Torm, who, pacing the harvester, made an athletically skillful mount. Lastly, Atuarre and Pakka came aboard, the cub clinging to his mother's tail. Blue Max accelerated for the spaceport perimeter.

Rekkon still held Han to the catwalk, but now it was to make sure he wouldn't fall. "Captain, you must accept that there's no more you can do here. Your chances of getting to Chewbacca here on Orron III are vanishing small. And, more to the point, it's doubtful he'll be here for long. Surely he'll be taken for interrogation, just like the others. Our mission is yours now; it's nearly certain the Wookiee will be put in with the rest of the Authority's special enemies."

Han wiped blood from his forehead, pulled himself upright, and began climbing a maintenance ladder.

"Where are you going?" Rekkon demanded.

"Someone has to tell Max where he's going," Han answered.

The spaceport was guarded by a security fence of fine mesh, ten meters high, carrying a lethal charge maintained by transmitting posts along its length. An unprotected man, or even an armored one, would stand no chance of making it through, but the harvester offered a special form of protection.

"Everybody get to a catwalk," Rekkon called.

102

"Stand on the insulated strips!" His various companions, Han included, rushed for positions, bracing their feet on the thick runners of insulation on the mechanic's catwalks.

The harvester hit the field area as Max threw his cutter blades into motion again. Defensive energy spat and spattered all around the agrirobot, discharging across its bow in skittering strands. Then the fence was torn apart by the harvester's blades, a twenty-meter length of it ripped loose and engulfed. The defensive field faded along that part of the fence, its continuity broken. Whereupon the giant machine churned out onto the flat, press-bonded landing area.

Han hauled himself up and looked down at Max, nestled in the control niche. "Can you program this crate so it'll run without you?"

The computer probe's photoreceptor swiveled around, coming up to bear on him. "That's what it's built to do, but it'll remember only simple things, Captain. For a machine it's pretty dumb."

Han weighed his suspicions, presumptions, and a knowledge of security procedures. "They'll be rushing their men to the passenger-ship end of the port; they won't think the barges are any good to us. But they'll certainly be looking for this tub, Max. Set it up so it'll give us a few seconds to get clear, then head itself down toward the main port area." To the others, he called, "Checkout time! Everybody pound ground!"

From Blue Max came low buzzes, beeps, and wonks of his labors. Then he announced, "Done, Captain, but we better get off right now."

Han reached down as Max disengaged himself from the harvester's controls, pulled free the connector jacks Chewbacca had inserted, and lifted the computer out of the niche. There was a carrying strap in a recessed groove on Max's top. Han pulled it out and slung Max over his shoulder.

When he reached the ground, Rekkon and the others were already there. They all stepped back as the harvester ground into motion again, wheeled promptly, and tore off between rows of barges. From the harvester, Han had already spotted, not far away, the barge shell concealing the *Millennium Falcon*. He handed Blue Max back to Bollux and started for his ship at a dead run, with the rest keeping up as best they could.

The outer hatch, the makeshift one, wasn't dogged, of course. He pushed it aside, palmed the ramp and inner hatch open. Then he dashed to the cockpit and began swiping at controls, bringing his ship back to life, yelling: "Rekkon, say the word the second everybody's onboard, and hang onto your heirlooms!" He pulled on his headset and deserted all caution, thinking, *Hell with preflight.* He brought the barge's engines up to full power all at once, and simply hoped they wouldn't blow or dummy out on liftoff.

His best hope lay in the nature of bureacracy. Somewhere back in the fields, the Espo detachment commander was trying to explain to his superior what had happened. That man, in turn, would have to contact port security and give them the rundown. Given a creaky enough chain of command, the *Falcon* still stood a chance.

Han pulled on his flight gloves and ran through his preparations with a sharp feeling of incompleteness; he was used to dividing the tasks with Chewbacca, and each detail of the liftoff drove home the fact that his friend wasn't there.

He checked the barge's readouts—and swore several of his choicer curses. Bollux, stumping into the cockpit to relay Rekkon's word that all was secure, added, "What's wrong, Captain?"

"The motherless barge is what's wrong! Some overeager Authority expediter filled it up already!" The instruments proved it; several hundred thousand metric tons of grain were stowed in the barge's vast shell. There went Han's plan for rapid ascent.

"But, sir," Bollux asked in his unhurried speech pattern, "can't you release the barge shell?"

"If the explosive-releases worked, and *if* I didn't damage the *Falcon,* I'd still have to get above the port's close-proximity defenses, and maybe a picket

ship." He turned and yelled back down the passageway, "Rekkon! Get somebody in those gun turrets; we may have to stand tall!" Han could operate the ship's top and belly turrets by means of servos from the cockpit, but remote control was a poor substitute for sentient gunners. "And screw your navels in; we go in twenty seconds!" He fumed over the fact that the barge's engines took so much longer to heat up than the *Falcon*'s.

Port control, having noticed that the barge was preparing to lift, began transmitting to what it still presumed to be a robotized ship orders to abort liftoff. Han hit the overrides and had the barge's computer answer by acknowledging clearance as if it had received permission to go. Port control repeated the command to hold, convinced it was dealing with a computer malfunction along with all its other problems.

Han brought the engines up. The barge wallowed up from its pit, bending aside the boarding gantry, ignoring all directions to do otherwise. As his radius of vision increased with altitude, Han spied the abandoned harvester. It was halfway to the other end of the giant port, surrounded by Espo hover-vans, skimmers, and self-propelled artillery. The harvester had been partially disabled, but still obeyed its preset programming mindlessly, trying to grind forward.

As Han watched, a cannonade from all sides stopped the huge machine for good, gouging large chunks from it, turning most of the harvester's lower chassis into wreckage. Someone no longer cared whether prisoners were taken or not. The harvester's power plant went up in a fireball, and the harvester split in half with a force that rocked the Espo field pieces back.

As the barge rose higher, responding sluggishly under its burden of cargo, ignoring chatter from the port control, Han saw the place where Chewbacca had been captured. Other Espo vehicles were gathered near the wreck of the hovervan. Han couldn't tell whether his partner was there or had already been taken away, but the fields were crawling with Security

Police, like a pestilence among the golden-red grain, searching for possible stragglers. Rekkon had been right; going back would've spelled certain disaster.

The barge gave a sudden, convulsive shudder, and the *Falcon*'s passengers felt as if someone had caught them by the collar and given a yank. With an ominous feeling, Han punched up the rear screens. Bollux, having nearly fallen, lowered himself into the navigator's chair, inquiring what was wrong. Han ignored him.

It *had* been a picket ship, in transpolar orbit, that he and Chewbacca had picked up just prior to landing. Even Rekkon hadn't realized how security-minded the Authority was about Orron III. Moving up hard astern the barge was a dreadnaught, one of the military's old Invincible Class capital ships—over two kilometers long, bristling with gun turrets, missile tubes, tractor-beam projectors, and deflector shields, armored like a protosteel mountain. The dreadnaught hailed them with the demand that the barge halt, and at the same time identified herself: the *Shannador's Revenge*. She'd locked her tractors onto the barge, and compared with her raw power, the lighter's beam back on Duroon had been a mere beckoning finger.

"Church is out," Han observed, bringing his ordnance up to charge and preparing to angle deflector shields, for all the good it would do. The dreadnaught had enough weaponry to hold and vaporize a score of ships like the *Falcon*. Han opened the intercom. "That shake-up was a tractor. Everybody stay cool—things could get rough." As if we have a prayer, he finished to himself. But he had no intention of being caught alive. Better to shorten a few Espo careers, and go out in style.

There were sounds of banging, tearing metal from the barge shell, of parting supports and struts. Some of the superstructural features, weakened or loosened by alterations to the hull, had been pulled free by the tractor beam and gone flying back toward the *Shannador's Revenge*.

Han took inspiration from it. He had at his side breadboarded computer overrides for the barge's every function. His fingers stabbed at them as he shouted, "Everybody brace! We're gonna—" and was slammed back in his seat. He'd hit the cargo release, opening the barge's rear dump-doors. Hundreds of thousands of tons of grain were poured into the dreadnaught's tractors, pulled toward the *Shannador's Revenge* by her own brute power, fanning out in a blinding contrail, as the barge surged ahead with a lightening load.

The dreadnaught was engulfed, her sensors muffled by the tidal wave of grain. Han, with one eye on his own sensors, saw that the warship was driving straight on through the hail of grain, closing quickly on the barge even though she was blinded. Her tractor beams were still clamped onto the barge's stern, and Han wondered how long it would be before her skipper gave the command to open fire.

There was only one other possibility. He hit the controls, cutting in the barge's retrothrusters, and with virtually the same motion, slapped the emergency releases. His other hand hovered over the main drive control of the *Millennium Falcon*.

The barge shell shook, losing much of its velocity, while the reports of exploding bolts sounded through both the freighter and the larger ship around it. Superstructural elements, added to secure the *Falcon* and disguise her lines, were blown clear. A split second later, the *Falcon*'s engines howled to life, their blue fire tearing the smaller ship free of the breakaway supports holding her and severing her external control hookups.

Han took the *Falcon* on the same course he'd been holding, keeping the barge shell between himself and the Authority warship. The *Shannador's Revenge*, her sensors impaired, had failed to note the barge shell's drastic drop in speed. The dreadnaught's captain was calling for a vector change just as the warship rammed the decelerating barge. The *Shannador's Revenge*'s forward screens flared with impact, and her anticoncussion fields cut in instantly on collision, as she cut the floating hulk of the barge shell in half in a terrific impact and suffered structural damage of her own. The warship's forward sensor suite was disabled; she resounded with alarms and damage reports. Airtight doors began booming shut automatically, triggered by decompressive hull ruptures.

The *Millennium Falcon* was clawing for the upper atmosphere. The thought that he'd bloodied the nose of a battlewagon, escaping against all odds, didn't lighten Han's mood, nor did the thought that hyperspace and safety were only moments away. Occupying his mind was one simple, intolerable fact: his friend and partner was now in the merciless hands of the Corporate Sector Authority.

When the stars had parted before him and the ship was safely in hyperspace, Han sat for long minutes thinking that he couldn't remember the last time he'd spaced without the Wookiee beside him. Rekkon had been right in arguing for escape, but that didn't change Han's feeling that he'd let Chewbacca down.

But regrets were a waste of time. Han stripped off his headset and shoved himself out of his seat. Rekkon was his only hope now. He headed for the forward compartment, the ship's combination lounge-mess-rec area, and realized something was wrong while he was still in the passageway. There was the pungent smell of ozone, the smell of blaster fire.

"Rekkon!"

Han ran to where the scholar slumped over the gameboard. He'd been shot from behind, by a blaster set on needle-beam at low power. The sound of it probably hadn't even carried across the compartment. On the gameboard, under Rekkon's body, was a portable readout. Next to it a clear puddle of molten liquid bubbled, the remains of the data plaque. Rekkon was dead, of course; he'd been shot at close range.

Han leaned on a bulkhead pad, rubbing his eyes and wondering what to do next. Rekkon had been his sole hope for rescuing Chewbacca and for getting himself out of this insane jam. With Rekkon dead, the hard-won information gone, and at least one traitor-murderer onboard, Han felt alone for one of the few times in his life. His blaster was in his hand, but there was no one else in the compartment or in the passageway.

A clattering on the rungs of the main ladderwell. Han ran to it just as Torm came climbing up from the *Falcon*'s belly turret. As he came up, Torm found himself staring into the muzzle of Han's gun.

"Just give over your pistol, Torm. Keep your right hand on the rung, and do it with your left, easy. Don't make a mistake; it'd be your one and only."

When he had the other man's weapon, Han let him ascend, then made him shuck his tool belt. Patting him down and finding no other weapons, Han motioned for him to move into the lounge, then called up the ladderwell for Atuarre to come down from the ship's top quad-mount.

He kept one eye on Torm, who was staring in shock at Rekkon's body. "Where's her cub?" he asked the man quietly.

The redhead shrugged. "Rekkon told Pakka to look around for a medi-pack. You weren't the only one who was injured along the way. The cub went off to rummage around. I guess when you yelled for everyone to stay put and hang on, he did." He looked back to Rekkon, as if he couldn't fathom the fact of the man's death. "Who did it, Solo? You?"

"No. And the list of possibilities is awfully short." He heard Atuarre's light tread on the rungs and covered her as she came down the ladderwell.

The Trianii's features became a mask of feline hatred. "You dare point a weapon at me?"

"Gag it. Toss your gun out here, careful, then step out and drop the tool belt. Somebody's killed Rekkon, and it could be you as easy as anyone. So don't push me. I'm not telling you twice."

Her eyes were wide now, the news of Rekkon's death appearing to shock her out of her fury. But how can I tell if it's real or an act? Han asked himself.

When he had them both in the forward compartment, he still found he couldn't pick up anything but shock and dismay. Theirs, at least, served to prod him out of his own.

A clanking on the deckplates marked Bollux's arrival from the cockpit. Han didn't look around until he heard the urgency in the 'droid's voice.

"Captain!"

Han whirled, dropping to one knee, blaster up. Beyond the cockpit offshoot from the passageway crouched the cub, Pakka, his small pistol held in one paw-hand, a medi-pack swinging from the other. He seemed to be wavering indecisively.

"He thinks you're threatening me!" Atuarre rasped, moving toward her cub. Han swung his blaster to cover her and looked back to the cub. "Tell the kid to drop it and come to you, Atuarre. Do it!"

She did, and the cub, shifting his wide eyes between Han and his mother, obeyed.

Torm took the medi-pack from the cub and handed it to Han. Still covering his passengers, Han moved to an acceleration chair and opened the pack with his free hand. He held the nozzle of an irrigation bulb against his forehead injury, then wiped at it with a disinfectant pad.

Putting the medi-pack down, he took up the three confiscated weapons, put them aside, and confronted Torm, Atuarre, and Pakka. His mind ran in circles. How to tell who had done it? They'd each had a weapon, and time. Either Pakka had doubled back from his search, or one of the others had left his turret long enough to murder. Han almost regretted not having exchanged fire with the *Shannador's Revenge;* at least he'd have known if either of the quad-mounts was untended.

Atuarre and Torm were trading suspicious looks now. "Rekkon told me," Torm was saying, "that he took you and the cub on against his better judgment."

"Me?" she shrilled. "What about you?" She turned to Han. "Or, for that matter, *you?*"

That shook him. "Sister, I'm the one who got you out of there, remember? Besides, how could I lift off and shoot Rekkon at the same time? And anyway, Bol-

110

lux was with me." Han rummaged again in the medi-pack, dug out a patch of synth-flesh, and pressed it over his injury, his mind in a turmoil.

"That all could've been done by computer, Solo, or you could have killed him just before I came down," Torm said. "And what good's a 'droid for a witness? You're the one pointing the blaster around, hotshot."

Han, pushing the medi-pack aside, replied, "I'll tell you what: you're all, all three of you, going to keep an eye on one another, and I'm going to be the only one with a gun. If anybody has the wrong look on his face, it's going to be all over for him. You're all fair game, understand?"

Atuarre moved to the gameboard. "I'll help you with Rekkon."

"Keep your hands off him," Torm shouted. "It was either you or that cub who killed him, maybe both." The big redhead's fists were bailed. Both Atuarre and Pakka were showing their fangs.

Han cut them off with a wave of the blaster. "Everybody relax. *I'll* take care of Rekkon; Bollux can help. The three of you move down to that cargo hold off the main passageway." He stifled their objections with a motion of the gun's muzzle. First Torm, then the two Trianii, began to move.

Han stood to one side as they filed into the empty hold. "If anybody sticks his face out of here without my say-so, I'll figure he's out to get me, and I'll fry him. And if anybody's hurt in here, I'll space whoever is left, no questions asked." He closed the hatch and left them.

In the forward compartment, Bollux waited silently, with Blue Max on a console nearby. Han regarded the corpse. "Well, Rekkon, you did your best, but it didn't get you far, did it? And you dumped it into my lap. Now my partner's captured and your murderer's onboard with me. You weren't a bad old man, but I somehow wish I'd never heard of you."

Han picked up one heavy arm, dragging at the corpse. "Bollux, you get ready to take the other side; he was no lightweight."

Then he noticed the scrawl. Han pushed Rekkon's body back clumsily and bent to examine a stylus's scribble on the gameboard that the dead man's arm had hidden. The writing was difficult to read, dashed off in a pained, distorted hand, hastily and weakly. Han turned his head this way and that, puzzling the message out aloud: "Stars' End, Mytus VII." He knelt and quickly found Rekkon's bloodstained stylus on the floor by the gameboard base. With his last strength, after he'd been left for dead, Rekkon had managed to leave word of what the computer plaque had told him. Dying, he hadn't abandoned his campaign.

"Foolish," Han told himself. "Who was he trying to tell?"

"You, Captain Solo," Bollux answered automatically. Han turned on him in surprise.

"What?"

"Rekkon left the message for you, sir. The wound indicates that he was shot from behind, and therefore quite probably never saw his assailant. The only living entity he could trust would be you, Captain, and it would be logical to assume you would be present when his body was moved. He made sure in this manner that the information would reach you."

Han stared down at the body for a long moment. "All right, you stubborn old man; you win." He reached over, smearing and eradicating the words with his hand. "Bollux, you never saw this, understand? Play dumb."

"Shall I erase that portion of my memory, sir?"

Han's answer was slow, as if he was catching the habit from the 'droid. "No. You may be the one who'll have to pass it along if I don't hack it. Make sure Blue Max keeps zipped, too."

"Yes, Captain." Bollux moved to take Rekkon's other arm as Han prepared to hoist again. His joints creaked, and his servos whined. "This was a great man, was he not, Captain?"

Han strained under the corpse's weight. "What d'you mean?"

"Just, sir, that he had a function, a purpose he cared about above and beyond his life. Doesn't that indicate a greatness to the purpose?"

"You'll have to read the obituaries, Bollux; all I can tell you is, he's dead. And we're going to have to eject him through the emergency lock; we might get boarded yet, and we can't have him around."

Without further conversation, the two dragged at Rekkon, who had reached out from beyond death and given Han the answers he needed.

Han opened the hatch. Atuarre, Pakka, and Torm looked up in unison. They'd taken seats on the bare deck, the man at the opposite side of the empty hold from the two Trianii.

"We had to ditch Rekkon," Han told them. "Atuarre, I want you and Pakka to go square away the forward compartment. You can throw some eats into the warming unit, too. Torm, come with me; I need a hand repairing the damage we did on liftoff."

Atuarre objected. "I am a Trianii Ranger, and a rated pilot, not a drudge. Besides, Solo-Captain, that man is a traitor."

"Save it," Han cut her off. "I've locked up all the other weapons in the ship, including Chewie's other bowcaster. I'm the only one armed, and things stay that way until I figure out what to do with you all."

She gave him a sullen look, telling him, "Solo-Captain, you're a fool." She left, with Pakka trailing behind.

Torm rose, but Han stopped him with an arm across the hatchway. The redhead retreated back into the hold and waited. "You're the only one I can trust," Han told him. "Bollux isn't really much good, and I just figured out who killed Rekkon."

"Which of them did it?"

"The cub, Pakka. He was in Authority custody, and they messed with him. That's why he doesn't talk. I think they brain-set him, then let Atuarre recover him. Rekkon wouldn't have let any of you others near."

Torm nodded grimly. Han produced the man's pistol from the back of his gunbelt and handed it to him. Its charge indicator read full. "Keep this on you. I'm not sure Atuarre's figured it out yet, but I'm willing to play them along and find out if either of them know anything that'll help."

Torm stashed the gun in his coverall pocket. "What will we do next?"

"Rekkon left a message as he was dying, scrawled it on the gameboard. The Authority's keeping its special prisoners at something called Stars' End, on Mytus VI. After we've checked the ship over, we'll gather in the forward compartment and run down everything we've got in files and computers on it. Maybe Pakka or Atuarre will let something slip then."

When the light damage suffered by the *Millennium Falcon* in her breakout from Orron III had been repaired insofar as was possible, the ship's complement gathered in the forward compartment. Han had brought four portable readouts. He gave one to each of the others and took one himself. Bollux watched, seated to one side, with Max back in his usual place, gazing out from the 'droid's chest.

"I patched these readouts into the ship's computers," Han explained. "Each of them's keyed to one kind of information. I'll pull navigational, Atuarre's got planetological; Pakka can retrieve the Authority's unclassified stuff, and Torm's got operational files from the outlaw-techs. Okay, punch up Stars' End and let's get at it."

Each of the other three complied. Torm's screen, except for the retrieval request, remained blank. Atuarre's too. She looked up, as they all did, to see Han scan his own readout.

"Your portables aren't hooked up to anything," he told them, "only mine. Atuarre, show Torm your screen."

Dubious, she still did as he asked, turning her readout so that the redhead could see it. On her screen was the simple retrieval request, MYTUS VIII. "Yours too, Pakka," Han bade the cub. That readout showed MYTUS V.

"Catch his face," Han told the others, meaning Torm, who had become pallid. "You know what you've done, don't you, Torm? Show everybody your readout. It says MYTUS VII, but I told you that Stars' End was on MYTUS VI, just as I told the others the wrong planet. But you already knew the right one, because you read it over Rekkon's shoulder before you killed him, right?" His voice lost its false lightness. "I said right, *traitor?*"

Torm jumped to his feet with impressive speed, gun drawn. Atuarre pulled her out too, and pointed it at him. But neither Torm's shot at Han nor Atuarre's at him worked.

"Two malfunctions?" Han inquired innocently, unlimbering the blaster at his side. "I betcha mine works, Torm."

Torm heaved his pistol wildly. Han reacted with a star pilot's reflexes, slapping the gun out of midair with his left hand. But Torm had already whirled and seized the surprised Atuarre in a savage infighting hold, prepared to break her neck with a slight twist. When she started to resist, he forced her neck to the brink of fracture, making her subside.

"Put down the blaster, Solo," he grated, "and get your hands on the gameboard, or I'll—"

He was interrupted as Pakka, in a spectacular leap, landed on Torm's shoulders, sinking fangs into his neck, clawing at his eyes, wrapping a supple tail around the traitor's throat. Torm was forced to release his hold to keep from being blinded. Atuarre sought to turn and fight, and even Bollux had risen in the moment of crisis, unsure of just what to do.

Torm gave Atuarre a vicious kick. His superior weight and strength sent her sprawling, blocking Han, who had been moving for a clear shot. As Han skirted Atuarre, Torm tore Pakka from his shoulders and threw the cub aside just as Bollux blundered into the pilot's path. Pakka bounced off one of the pads of

115

safety cushioning lining the compartment hatch, as Torm dashed into the passageway.

Dodging, moving as quickly as he could, Torm raced past the cockpit, main ladderwell, and ramp hatch; none of them held any promise of even temporary safety. He heard Han's bootsteps close behind and ducked into the first compartment he came to, damning himself for not having taken time to learn the ship's layout. He hit the hatch-close button as he came through. The compartment was empty, offering no tools, nothing he might use as a weapon. He'd been hoping this was the escape-pod chamber, but fortune had passed him by. At least, he thought, he had a moment's respite. He might be able to buy time, perhaps even wrest Solo's blaster from him. His thoughts were moving so quickly that he didn't realize, for a moment, where he was. But when he did, he threw himself back at the hatch through which he'd come, tearing at the controls, screaming obscenities.

"Don't waste your time," came Han's voice over the intercom. "Nice of you to choose the emergency lock, Torm. It's where you would've ended up anyway."

Han stood looking through the viewport set in the lock's inner hatch. He'd overridden the lock's controls to make sure Torm couldn't get back in. All the *Falcon*'s access systems had inboard overrides, to make life complicated for anyone interested in forced entry, a wise smuggler's option.

Torm tried to wet his lips with a very dry tongue. "Solo, stop and think a minute."

"Save your breath, Torm. You're gonna need it all; you're going swimming." There were, of course, no spacesuits stored in the lock. Torm's eyes opened wide with fear.

"Solo, no! I never had anything against you; I never would have come, except that bastard Rekkon and the Trianii never took their eyes off me. If I'd cut, they would have shot me. You can understand that, can't you? I had to look out for number one, Solo!"

"So you shot Rekkon," Han told him in a soft voice, no questioning to it.

"I had to! If he'd passed on word about Stars' End, it would've been my neck! You don't know these Authority people, Solo; they don't accept failure. It was Rekkon or me."

Atuarre came up behind Han, and Pakka and Bollux after her. The cub climbed up the 'droid's shoulders for a better view. "But, Torm," Atuarre said, "Rekkon found you, recruited you. Your father and brother really have disappeared."

Without facing away from the viewport, Han added, "I'm sure they did. Your father and older brother, right, Torm? Let's see, now, that wouldn't by any chance make you heir to the Kail Ranges, would it?"

The traitor's face was waxen. "Yes, if I did as the Authority asked. Solo, don't play righteous with me! You said you're a businessman, didn't you? I can get all the money you want! You want your friend back? The Wookiee is on his way to Stars' End by now; the only way you'll ever see him again is by bargaining with me. The Authority's got no grudge against you; you can name your price!"

Torm reasserted control over himself, going on more calmly. "These people keep their word, Solo. They don't even know your names yet, any of you; I was operating under deep cover, saving the information I developed so I could up the price. Strike a deal. The Authority's just good business people, like you and me. You can have the Wookiee back and go free with enough money to buy a new ship."

He got no answer. Han's gaze had gone to his own reflection in the metal of the emergency lock's control panel. Torm pounded his fists on the inner hatch, a dull thudding.

"Solo, tell me what you want; I'll get it for you, I swear! You're a guy who looks out for number one, aren't you? *Isn't that what you are, Solo?*"

Han stared at his own lean reflection. In another man, he'd have said those eyes were too used to concealing everything but cynicism. His thoughts echoed Torm: *Is that what I am?* He looked back to Torm's face, straining against the viewport.

"Ask Rekkon," Han answered, and hit the lock release.

The outer hatch snapped open. With an explosion of air into vacuum, Torm was hurled out into the chaotic pseudoreality of hyperspace. Once outside the *Millennium Falcon*'s mantle of energy, the units of matter and patterns of force that had been Torm ceased to have any coherent meaning.

 VIII

"SOLO-CAPTAIN," Atuarre interrupted his thoughts, leaning into the cockpit, "isn't it time we spoke? We've been here for nearly ten Standard Time-Parts, and our course of action is no clearer than when we arrived. We must reach some decision, don't you agree?"

Han broke off gazing out the canopy at the distant speck, barely visible, of Mytus VII. All around the *Millennium Falcon* rose the peaks and hills of the tiny asteroid on which she was concealed. "Atuarre, I don't know how Trianii feel about waiting, but me, I hate it worse than anything. But there's nothing else we can do; we have to sit tight and play out our hand."

She wouldn't accept that. "There are other courses of action, Captain. We could attempt to contact Jessa again." Her slit-irises dwelled on him.

Han shifted around in the pilot seat to face her directly, so quickly that she drew back reflexively. Seeing this, he reined in his temper. "We could waste all kinds of time looking for Jessa. When her operation ran, after we got hit by the IRDs, she probably dug a hole and pulled it in after her. The *Falcon* can cook along at point-five factors over Big L, but we still might waste a month looking for the outlaw-techs and not find them. Maybe word will find its way to Jessa, or one of the prearranged blind transmissions, but we can't bank on her. I don't count on anybody but me; if I have to bust Chewie out of there alone, I'll do it."

Some of the tension left her. "You aren't alone, Solo-Captain. My mate is there at Stars' End, too. Your fight is Atuarre's." She extended a slim, sharp-clawed hand. "But come, now, take some food. Staring at Mytus VII cannot help and may be distracting us from solutions."

He pushed himself up out of the seat, taking one more look at the distant planet. Mytus VII was a worthless rock, as worlds went, revolving around a small, unexceptional sun at the end of the wisp of stars that was the Corporate Sector. Stars' End, indeed. There'd be scant danger of anyone's happening on the Authority's secret prison facility here, unless he came looking for it specifically.

Since Mytus VII had been listed in the charts as being at the outermost edge of its solar system, Han had broken into normal space nearly ten Standard Time-Parts before, deep in interstellar space, far out of sensor range. He'd come in from the opposite side of the system, entering a thick asteroid belt halfway between Mytus VII and its sun, and hunted up what he'd wanted, this jagged hunk of stone. Using his starship's engines and tractors, he'd brought the asteroid onto a new course, one that would allow him to take a long-range peek at Stars' End, sure that no one there would notice the slightly unusual behavior of one tiny mote in the uncharted asteroid belt.

He'd spent most of his time monitoring the planet's communications, studying it by sensors, and watching the occasional ship come and go. Monitored commo traffic had told him nothing; most of it had been encrypted in codes that had resisted his computers' analyses. Plaintext messages had been either mundane or meaningless, and Han suspected that at least some of them had been sent strictly for appearances' sake, to make Stars' End look like an ordinary, if remote, Authority installation.

Now he trailed Atuarre into the forward compartment. Bollux was seated near the gameboard, his plastron open. Pakka was stalking a jetting remote back and forth. The remote, a small globe powered by magnetic fields and repulsor power, turned, dove, climbed, and dodged unpredictably. The cub hunted it with tail twitching and quivering, obviously enjoying the game. The remote eluded him time and again, demonstrating more than its usual maneuverability.

As Han watched, Pakka nearly caught the globe, but it evaded his pounce at the last second. Han looked to the 'droid. "Bollux, are you directing that remote?"

The red photoreceptors trained on him. "No, Captain. Max is sending information pulses to it. He's much better at anticipation and dictating random factors than I, sir. Random factors are extremely difficult concepts."

Han watched the cub make a final, long spring and catch the remote in midair, pulling it to the deck and rolling over and over with it in sheer delight. Then the pilot sat at the gameboard, which often doubled as a table, and accepted a mug of concentrate broth from Atuarre. They had used up fresh supplies several Time-Parts before and were now sustaining themselves on the *Falcon*'s ample, if bland, emergency rations.

"There have been no new developments, Captain?" Bollux asked. Han presumed the 'droid already knew the answer and had asked only out of a sort of programmed conversational courtesy. Bollux had turned out to be an entertaining shipmate who could spin hours of tales and accounts of his long years' work and the many worlds he'd seen. He also had a repertoire of jokes programmed into him by a former owner, and an absolutely deadpan delivery.

"Zero, Bollux. Absolutely zilch."

"May I suggest, sir, that you assemble all available information in sum, recapping it? Among sentient life forms, new ideas sometimes emerge that way, I have noticed."

"I bet. After all, aren't most decrepit labor 'droids armchair philosophers?" Han put his mug down, rubbing his jaw thoughtfully. "Anyway, there isn't much to tote up. We're on our own—"

"Are you sure there's no other resource?" Max chirped.

"Don't start that again, lowpockets," Han warned. "Where was I? We've found the place we want, Mytus VII, and—"

"How high is the order of probability?" Max wanted to know.

"Up an afterburner with the order of probability," Han snapped. "If Rekkon said it's here, it's here. The installation has a pretty big power plant, almost fortress class. And quit interrupting, or I'll take a drill to you.

"Let's see. We can't hang around forever, either; supplies are running low. What else?" He scratched his forehead where the synth-flesh patch had flaked away, leaving new, unscarred skin.

"This is a strictly off-limits solar system," Atuarre contributed.

"Oh, yeah, and if we get nailed here without a mighty good alibi, they'll stick *us* in jail, or whatever." He smiled at Bollux and Blue Max. "Except you boys. You, they'd probably recycle into lint filters and spittoons."

He dragged the toe of his boot back and forth on the deck. "Not much more to it; only that I'm not leaving this stretch of space without Chewie." Of all the things he'd mentioned, he was surest of that. He'd spent many long watches in the *Falcon*'s cockpit, haunted by what his Wookiee partner might be undergoing. A hundred times since taking up this vigil, he'd almost cut in the ship's engines to shoot his way into Stars' End and get his friend out or get flamed in the attempt. Each time, his hand had been stayed by the memory of Rekkon's words, but it was a constant struggle for Han to restrain his impulses.

Atuarre had plainly been thinking along the same lines. "When the Espos came to evict us from our colony world," she said slowly, "some Trianii tried armed resistance. The Espos were brutal in their interrogation of prisoners, seeking the ringleaders. It was the first time I had seen anyone use The Burning. You know what I refer to, Solo-Captain?"

Han did. The Burning was a torture involving the use of a blaster set at low power, to scorch and sear the flesh off a prisoner, leaving only blood-smeared bone. Usually, a leg would be first, immobilizing the victim; then the rest of the skeleton was exposed, inch by inch. Any other prisoners could be made to watch, to break their will. The Burning seldom failed to obtain answers, if answers were to be had; but in Han's opinion, no being who employed such methods deserved to live.

"I will not leave my mate in the hands of the kind of people who would do that," Atuarre was saying. "We are Trianii; death, if it comes to that, is not something we fear."

"Not a very linear analysis," Blue Max piped up.

"Well, who said *you'd* understand it, birdhouse?" Han scoffed.

"Oh, I comprehend it, Captain," Max said with what Han could've sworn was a note of pride. "I just said it wasn't very—"

He was interrupted by a beep from the commo monitoring suite. Han was out of his chair and halfway to the cockpit by the second beep. Just as he slid into the pilot's seat, a last, sustained beep signaled the end of the transmission.

"The recorder bagged it," Han said, hitting the playback. "I don't think it was encrypted."

It was a cleartext message, sent economically, in burst. He had to slow down the playback by a five-to-one factor before it ungarbled.

"To: Corporate Vice-President Hirken, Authority

facility at Stars' End," the audio-reconstruction began. "From: the Imperial Entertainers' Guild. We beg the Viceprex's indulgence and forgiveness, but the troupe scheduled to stop at your location has been forced to cancel its itinerary because of transportational mishap. This office will schedule a replacement immediately, when a troupe with a 'droid of the requisite type becomes available. I am, distinguished Viceprex, your abject servant, Hokkor Long, Secretary in charge of scheduling, Imperial Entertainers' Guild."

Han's fist hit the console on the last syllable. "That's it!"

Atuarre's expression mixed befuddlement with doubt of Han's soundness of mind. "Solo-Captain, that's what?"

"No, no, I mean that's *us*. We're in! We just got dealt a wild card!"

He whooped, slammed his fist in his palm, and nearly ruffled Atuarre's thick mane from glee. She retreated a step. "Solo-Captain, has the oxygen pressure dropped too low for you? That message was about entertainers."

He snorted. "Where've you been all your life? He said *replacement* entertainers. Don't you know what that means? Haven't you ever seen the broken-down acts the Guild'll throw in to fill a playdate, just so they can hang on to their agent's fee? Haven't you ever gone to some bash where they promised a class act, then at the last second they pull a switch and stick in some . . ."

It dawned on him that they were all staring at him now, photoreceptors and Trianii eyes. He half sobered. "What else can we do? The only other thing I've thought of is to fly into Mytus VII backward so they'd think we were leaving. But this is even *wilier*. We can do it. Oh, they'll think we stink like banta droppings maybe, but they'll buy the lie."

He saw Atuarre was far from convinced, and turned to Pakka. "They want entertainers. How'd you like to be an acrobat?"

The cub made a little bounce, a kind of strain to

speak, then, frustrated, sprang into a backflip to swing upside down from an overhead control conduit by his knees and tail.

Han nodded approval. "What about it, Atuarre, for your mate's sake? Can you sing? Do magic tricks?"

She was nonplused, resenting his appeal to Pakka and his invocation of her mate. But she saw, too, that he was right. How many chances like this would come their way?

The cub began clapping his paws for Han's attention. When he got it, Pakka shook his head energetically in answer to Han's last question; then, still hanging upside down, he put paws on hips and made wriggling motions.

Han's eyebrows knit. "A . . . dancer? Atuarre, you're a dancer!"

She cuffed her cub's rump sharply. "I am not, er, unskilled in the rites of my people." Han saw she was embarrassed; she riveted him with a defiant stare. "And what of you, Solo-Captain? With what will you astonish your audience?"

He was too exhilarated with the prospect of action to be dampened. "Me? I'll think of something. Inspiration's my specialty!"

"A dangerous specialty, the most dangerous of all, perhaps. What of the 'droid? What 'droid? We don't even know what kind of 'droid they meant."

"Ah, a *replacement* 'droid, remember?" Han talked fast, to sell his point, gesturing at Bollux. The 'droid made strangely human prevocal sounds, a creak of astonishment, and Blue Max got out a "Wow!" as Han rattled on.

"We can say the Guild got it wrong. So Stars' End wanted a juggler or whatever and they get a storyteller. So what? We'll tell them to go sue the Entertainers' Guild!"

"Captain Solo, sir, if you please," Bollux finally interjected. "With your kind permission, sir, I must point out—"

But Han already had his hands on the 'droid's weatherbeaten shoulders, eyeing him artistically.

"Hmm, new paint, of course, and there's plenty aboard; it often pays to slap a coat on something before resale, especially if you didn't own it to begin with. Scarlet liqui-gloss, I think; a five-coat job's all we have time for. And maybe some trim. Nothing flashy, no scrollwork or filigree; just some restrained silver pinstriping. Bollux, boy, you can stop worrying about obsolescence after this, 'cause you're gonna lay 'em in the aisles!"

Their approach and planetfall were uneventful. Han had altered the drift of their captive asteroid to take him back out of range of the Authority's sensors and then abandoned it. Once back in deep space, he'd made a nanno-jump, barely brushing hyperspace, to emerge near Mytus VII and its two small moonlets.

The *Falcon* identified herself, using the Waivered registration obtained by Rekkon. To that was added the proud announcement that she was the grand touring vehicle of Madam Atuarre's Roving Performers.

Mytus VII was a place of rocky desolation, airless, its distance from its sun rendering it dim and cheerless. If anybody escaped Stars' End, he'd have no place to go; the rest of the solar system was untenanted, none of its planets being hospitable to humanoid life.

The Authority's installation was marked by groupings of temporary dormitories, hangars and guard barracks, hydroponics layouts, dome-sheds and weapons sites. The ground was gouged and pocked where construction of permanent subsurface facilities was in progress, but there was at least one finished structure already. In the middle of the base reared a tower like a stark, gleaming dagger.

Evidently no tunnel system had been completed yet. The whole complex was interconnected by a maze of tunnel-tubes, like giant, pleated hoses radiating from their boxy junction stations, a common arrangement for construction sites on airless worlds.

There was only one sizable vessel on the ground, an armed Espo assault craft. There were also smaller craft and unarmed cargo lighters, but Han had checked carefully for picket ships this time and was satisfied that there were none.

Han, checking visually for that heavyweight power plant his sensors had spotted, failed to locate it and wondered if it might be in that tower. He shot a second look at the tower, thinking something about it looked strange. It was equipped with two heavy docking locks, one at ground level and the other near its summit, the former hooked up to a tunnel-tube. He would very much have liked to run a close sweep of the place to see if he could pick up a high concentration of life forms that might indicate prisoners, but dared not for fear of counterdetection. Being caught probing the base would spell the end of the masquerade.

He made an undistinguished approach, nothing fancy, revealing none of the *Falcon*'s hidden capabilities. The attentive snouts of turbo-lasers tracked the ship exactingly. Ground control guided the starship down, and one of the tunnel-tubes snaked out, its folded skin extended by its servoframe, its hatch-mounted mouth sealing to the *Millennium Falcon*'s hull, swallowing the ship's lowering ramp.

Han shut down the engines. Atuarre, in the oversized copilot's seat, said, "I tell you one last time, Solo-Captain: I don't wish to be the one to do the speaking."

He brought his chair around. "I'm no actor, Atuarre. It'd be different if we were just going to jump in, spring the prisoners, and kiss off, but I can't cut all that chitchat and play the role."

They left the cockpit. Han was wearing a tight-cut black body suit, converted into a costume by the addition of epaulets, piping, shining braid, and a broad yellow sash, over which he'd buckled his blaster. His boots were newly polished.

Atuarre was bedecked at wrists, forearms, throat, forehead, and knees with bunches of multicolored streamers, Trianii attire for festivals and joyful occasions. She'd applied the exotic perfumes and formal scents of her species, using up the tiny supply she had in her belt pouch.

"I am no actress, either," she reminded him as they met the others at the ramp hatch.

"Did you ever see a celebrity?"

"Authority execs and their wives, when they came to our world as tourists."

Han snapped his fingers. "That's it. Smug, dumb, and happy."

Pakka was costumed as his mother was, wearing the scents appropriate to a pre-adolescent male. He handed his mother and Han long, billowing metallic capes, hers coppery and his an electric blue. Han's small wardrobe had been ransacked for material for the costumes, and the capes had come from the thin insulating layers of a tent from the ship's survival gear.

The fitting, seaming, and alternations had been a problem. Han was all thumbs when it came to tailoring, and the Trianii, of course, were a species who had never developed the art because they never wore anything but protective clothing. The solution had come in the form of Bollux, who had been programmed for the necessary skills, among others, while serving a regimental commander during the Clone Wars.

The ramp was already down; all that remained was to open the hatch. "Luck to us all," Atuarre bade them softly. They piled hands, including Bollux's cold metal ones, then Han reached for the switch.

As the hatch rolled up, Atuarre was still objecting. "Solo-Captain, I still think you ought to be the one to—" At the foot of the ramp, the tunnel-tube was crammed with body-armored Espos brandishing heavy blasters, riot guns, gas projectors, fusion-cutters, and sapper charges. Whirling, Atuarre gushed, "Oh, my! How thoughtful! My dears, they've sent us a guard of honor!"

She touched up her glossy, fine-brushed mane with one hand, smiling down at the Security Policemen charmingly. Han wondered why he'd ever worried.

The Espos, keyed up for a shootout, stared popeyed as she swept down the ramp, the profusion of streamers rippling and snapping behind her, her cape shimmering. Her steps sounded with the anklet-chimes that Han had run off for her from shipboard materials, using his small but complete tool locker.

At the front of the Espo ranks was a battalion commander, a major, his black swagger stick held behind his back, spine stiff, face rigid with officiousness. Atuarre descended the ramp as if she were receiving the keys to the planet, waving as if to acknowledge a standing ovation.

"My dear, *dear* General," she halfsang, intentionally giving the man a promotion, "I'm simply beyond words! Viceprex Hirken is too kind, I'm sure. And to you and your gallant men, thanks from Madam Atuarre and her Roving Performers!" She swooped right up to him, ignoring the guns and bombs and other items of destruction, one hand playing with the major's ribbons and medals, the other waving her gratitude to the massed, dumbfounded Espos. A dark, high-blood-pressure blush rose out of the major's collar and climbed swiftly for his hairline.

"What is the meaning of this?" he sputtered. "Are you saying you're the entertainers Viceprex Hirken is expecting?"

Her face showed cute confusion. "To be sure. You mean word of our arrival wasn't forwarded here to Stars' End? The Imperial Entertainers' Guild assured me it would communicate with you; I *always* demand adequate advanced billing."

She swept a grand gesture back up the ramp. "Gentlemen! Madam Atuarre presents her Roving Performers! First, Master Marksman, wizard of weaponry, whose target-shooting tricks and glittering gunplay have astounded audiences everywhere!"

Han walked down the ramp, trying to look the part, sweating under the tunnel-tube's worklights. Atuarre and the others could use their real names with impunity here, since those names had never appeared in Authority files. But Han's might have, and so he'd been forced into this new persona. He wasn't altogether sure he liked it now. When the Espos saw his blaster, weapons came up to cover him, and he was cautious to keep his hand away from it.

But Atuarre was already chattering. "And, to amaze and amuse you with feats of gymnastics and spellbinding acrobatics, Atuarre presents her pet prodigy—"

Han held up a hoop he had brought down with him. It was a ring-stabilizer off an old repulsor rig, but he'd plated it and fitted it with an insulated handgrip and a breadboarded distortion unit. Now he thumbed a switch, and the hoop became a circle of dancing light and waves of color as the distortion unit scrambled the visible spectrum, throwing off sparks and flares.

"—Pakka!" Atuarre introduced. The cub dived through the harmless light-effects, bounced off the ramp, and executed a triple forward somersault, into a double twist, and ended bowing deeply to the surprised major. Han scaled the hoop back into the ship and stepped to one side.

"And lastly," Atuarre went on, "that astonishing automaton, robotic raconteur, and machine of mirth and merriment, *Bollux!*"

And the 'droid clanked stiffly down the ramp, long arms swinging, somehow making it all look like a military march. Han had knocked out most of his dents and dings and applied a radiant paint job, five layers of scarlet liqui-gloss, as promised, with glinting silver pinstriping, painstakingly limned. The 'droid had been converted from an obsolescent into a classic. The mask-and-sunburst emblem of the Imperial Entertainer's Guild embellished one side of his chest, a touch that Han had thought would raise their credibility.

The Espo major was stumped. He knew Viceprex Hirken was expecting a special entertainment group, but was not aware of any clearance for one's arrival. Nevertheless, the Viceprex attached particular importance to his diversions and wouldn't take kindly to any meddling or delay. No, not kindly at all.

The major put on as cordial an expression as his gruff face could achieve. "I'll notify the Viceprex of your arrival at once, Madam, ah, Atuarre?"

"Yes, splendid!" She gathered her cape for a curtsy and turned to Pakka. "Fetch your props, my sweet." The cub skipped back up the ramp and returned a moment later with several hoops, a balance-ball, and an assortment of lesser props scrounged up aboard ship.

"I'll escort you to Stars' End," said the major. "And I'm afraid my men will have to hold on to your Master Marksman's weapon. You understand, Madam: Standard Operating Procedure."

Han steeled himself and handed his blaster over butt-first to an Espo sergeant as Atuarre nodded to the major. "Of course, of course. We must never ignore the proprieties, must we? Now, my dear, *dear* General, if you'd be so gracious . . ."

He realized with a start that she was waiting for his arm, and extended it stiffly, his face livid. The Espos, knowing their commanding officer's temper, hid their grins carefully. They formed up a hasty honor guard as Han hit the ramp control. The ramp pulled itself up quickly and the hatch rolled closed. They would reopen for no one but himself, Chewbacca, or one of the Trianii.

The major, after sending a runner ahead, led the group off through the tunnel-tube mazework. They were a long walk from the tower, and passed through several of the tread-mounted junction stations, to the surprised gazes of black-coveralled tech controlmen. Their footsteps and Bollux's clanking joints echoed through the tunnel-tubes, and the new arrivals noticed a gravity markedly lighter than the Standard gee maintained onboard the *Millennium Falcon*. Air in the tubes had the tang of hydroponics recycling, a welcome change from shipboard.

They came at last to a large, permanent air lock. Its outer hatch swung open at a verbal order from the major. Han caught a quick glimpse of what he knew must be the tower's side, surrounded by the tunnel-tube's seal, that confirmed something he'd thought he'd seen when landing.

Stars' End, or at least the tower's outer sheath, was molecularly bonded armor, of a single piece. That made it one of the most expensive buildings—no, he corrected himself, *the* most expensive building—Han had ever seen. Enhancing the molecular bonding of dense metals was a costly process, and doing it on this scale was something he'd simply never heard of.

Inside the tower, they passed down a long, broad corridor to the central axis, which was a service core that also housed elevator banks. They were hurried along, with little chance to gawk, but they did see techs, Authority execs, and Espos coming and going. Stars' End itself didn't appear to be particularly well manned, which didn't jell with the theory that it was a prison.

They entered an elevator with the major and a few of his men and were whisked upward in a high-speed ride. When the elevator opened and they trailed the major out, they found themselves standing beneath the stars, which shone so brightly and were packed so tightly overhead that they seemed more like a mist of light.

Then Han realized they were on top of Stars' End, which was covered with a dome of transparisteel. There was an apron of bright flooring by the elevators. Beyond that began a small glen, complete with miniature streamlet, and flowers and vegetation from many worlds, landscaped down to the last bud and leaf. He could hear the sounds of birds and small animals, the hum of pollinating insects, all of which were confined to the roof garden, he assumed, by partition fields. The glen was cleverly lit by miniature sun-globes of various colors.

Footsteps to their right made them turn. A man came around the curve of the tower's service core, a tall, handsome patriarch of a man. He wore superbly cut uppermost-exec's attire—a cutaway coat, formal vest, pleated shirt and meticulously creased trousers, set off by a jaunty red cravat. His smile was hearty and convincing, his hair white and full, his hands clean and soft, his nails manicured and lacquered. Han instantly wanted to bop him in the skull and dump him down the elevator shaft.

The man's voice was sure and melodious. "Welcome to Stars' End, Madam Atuarre. I am Hirken, Vice-President Hirken, of the Corporate Sector Authority. Alas, you come unheralded, or I'd have greeted you with greater pomp."

Atuarre feigned distress. "Oh, honorable sir, what shall I say? We were contacted by the Guild and asked to serve as a replacement act, at the last moment, as it were. But I was told the Secretary in charge of scheduling, Hokkor Long, would make all arrangements."

Viceprex Hirken smiled, a charming drawing back of red lips from chalk-white teeth. Han thought how useful that smile and smooth voice must be in Authority board sessions. "Totally unimportant," the Viceprex announced. "Your appearance is thus an unexpected pleasure."

"Why, how gracious of you! Never fear, my kind Vicprex; we'll distract you from the problems and pressures of your high office!" To herself, though, Atuarre swore Trianii vengeance: *If you've hurt my mate, I vow I'll see your living heart in my hand!*

Han observed that Hirken wore, at his belt, a small, flat instrument, a master-control unit. He assumed that the man liked to keep close watch on everything in Stars' End; the unit gave him total control of his domain.

"I have gathered some of the most prestigious entertainers in this part of our galaxy," Atuarre continued. "Pakka here is a premier acrobat, and I myself, in addition to being mistress of ceremonies, perform the traditional music and ritual dance of my people. And here stands our handsome Master Marksman, peerless expert with firearms, to amaze you, worshipful Viceprex, with his trick shooting."

There was a whistling laugh and a jeering: "Trick shooting of what? Of his mouth, as appears likely?"

The speaker appeared behind Viceprex Hirken. He

132

was a reptilian creature, slender and quick of movement. Viceprex Hirken chided the humanoid gently. "There, there, Uul; these good folks have come a long way to relieve our tedium." He turned to Atuarre. "Uul-Rha-Shan is my personal bodyguard, and something of an adept with weapons himself. Perhaps a contest of some sort could be arranged later. Uul has such a droll sense of humor, don't you agree?"

Han was eyeing the reptile, whose bright green scales were marked with diamond patterns of red and white, and whose big black, emotionless eyes were studying Han. Uul-Rha-Shan's jaw hung open a bit, exposing fangs and a restless pink tongue. Strapped to his right forearm was a pistol, a disrupter, Han thought, in a spring-loaded or power-driven holster of some kind.

Uul-Rha-Shan had taken up a position to Hirken's right. Han recalled having heard the bodyguard's name before. The galaxy was filled with species, all boasting their exceptional killers. Nonetheless, some individuals rose to a kind of prominence. One of those, an assassin and gunman who, it was said, would go anywhere and slay anyone for the right price, was Uul-Rha-Shan.

Hirken's manner had shifted to businesslike demeanor. "Now, that is the 'droid I requested, I take it?" He inspected Bollux unsmilingly, with a look that put cold danger in the air. "I was most specific with the Guild; I told Hokkor Long precisely what sort of 'droid I desired and stressed that they were to send nothing else. Has Long acquainted you with my desires?"

Atuarre swallowed, trying not to let her effusive manner slip. "Of a certainty, Viceprex, he did."

Hirken threw one more skeptical look at Bollux. "Very well. Follow me." He set off, back the way he had come, Uul-Rha-Shan at his heels. The travelers and their escort came behind. They left the garden area, coming to an amphitheater, an open expanse surrounded by banks of comfortable seats, separated by partitions of transparisteel.

"Automated fighting is combat at its purest, don't

you agree?" Hirken said chattily. "No living creature, no matter how savage, is free of the taint of self-preservation. But automata, ah! They are without regard for themselves, existing only to follow orders and destroy. My own combat-automaton is a Mark-X Executioner; there aren't many of them around. Has your gladiator 'droid ever fought one?"

Han's nerves were screaming; he was trying to figure out whom to jump for a weapon if, as he feared, Atuarre bobbled her reply. Any show of hesitation or ignorance now would surely tip their hand to Hirken and his men.

But she improvised smoothly. "No, Viceprex, not the Mark X."

Han was struggling with the jarring revelation. Gladiator 'droid? So that was what Hirken assumed Bollux was. Han had known, naturally, that matching 'droids and other automata in combat was a fad among the wealthy and jaded, but it hadn't occurred to him that Hirken would be among those. He put his brain into overdrive, looking for a way out.

As they walked, a woman joined them, coming from what was evidently a private lift tube. She was short, extremely fat, and trying to hide it with expensive, well-tailored robes. Han thought she looked as if somebody had draped a drogue parachute over an escape pod.

She took Hirken's hand. The Viceprex endured the gesture with ill humor. She fluttered a fat, beautifully maintained hand and chortled, "Oh, darling, do we have company?"

Hirken turned upon the woman a stare that, Han calculated, was enough to dissolve covalent bonding. The chubby birdbrain ignored it. The Viceprex gritted his teeth. "No, dearest. These people have brought a new competitor for my Mark X. Madame Atuarre and Company, I present my lovely bride, Neera. By the way, Madam Atuarre, what did you say your 'droid's designation is?"

Han jumped in. "He's one of a kind, um, Viceprex.

We designed him ourselves and call him Annihilator."
He turned to Bollux.

Bollux looked from Han to Hirken, then bowed.
"Annihilator, at your service. To destroy is to serve,
exalted sir."

"But our troupe has other acts to offer," Atuarre
was quick to tell Hirken's wife. "Tumbling, dancing,
trick shooting, and more."

"Ooh, dearest!" the obese woman exclaimed, clapping her hands, sliding up against her husband. "Let's
see that first! I grow so tired of watching that old Mark
X demolish other machinery. How boring and un-
couth and crude, really! And live performers would
be such a relief from those dreadful holotapes and re-
corded music. And we have company here so seldom."
She made puckering noises which, Han took it, were
intended to be kisses to her husband. Han thought
they sounded more like the attack of some inverte-
brate.

He saw a chance to solve two problems at once:
how to get Bollux out of the match and how to get a
look around Stars' End on his own. "Uh, honored
Viceprex, I'm also gaffer for the troupe. I have to tell
you, our gladiator 'droid, Annihilator there, was damaged in his last match. His auxiliary management
circuitry needs to be checked. If I could use your
shop, it'd only take a few minutes. You and your wife
could enjoy the other performances in the meantime."

Hirken looked up at the stars through the dome
and sighed, while his wife giggled and seconded the
proposal. "Very well. But make these repairs quickly,
Marksman. I'm not much taken with acrobats or dancing."

"Sure, right."

The Viceprex summoned a tech supervisor who had
been checking the amphitheater's systems and explained to the man what was needed. Then he offered
his arm, unwillingly, to his wife. They went to find
seats in the amphitheater, with the Espo major and his
men ranging themselves around in a loose guard formation. Uul-Rha-Shan, with a last, menacing look at

135

Han, followed along, again positioning himself near Hirken's right.

Since Pakka's acrobatics and Atuarre's dancing would pose no danger to the audience, Hirken hit a control on his belt unit, and the transparisteel slabs forming the arena's walls slid away into floor slots. The Viceprex and his wife settled into luxurious conform-loungers. Pakka readied his props.

Han turned to the supervisor tech who'd been placed at his disposal. "Wait for me by the elevator; I'll get the circuit box out, be with you in a second."

The man left. Han, loosening his cape and sliding it from his shoulders, turned to Bollux. "Okay, open up just enough for me to get Max."

The plastron opened partway. Han leaned close, shielded by the plastron halves. As he freed the computer-probe, he warned, "Not a sound, Max. You're supposed to be a combat-control component, so no funny stuff. You're deaf and dumb as of now." As a signal that he understood, Blue Max's photo-receptor went dim. "Good boy, Maxie."

Han straightened, slinging the computer's shoulder strap over his arm. As Bollux closed his chest up, Han handed his cape and gunbelt over and patted the 'droid's freshly painted head. "Hold these for me and stay loose, Bollux. This shouldn't take long."

As Han joined the tech supervisor at the elevator, Pakka was just beginning a marvelous exhibition of tumbling and gymnastics. The cub was a competition-class acrobat and covered the amphitheater floor in a series of flips, twists, and cartwheels, somersaulting through a hoop he held and, perching on the balance-ball, moving himself around the arena with both hands and feet. Then Atuarre came in to act as thrower as Pakka became a flyer.

Hirken's wife thought it all charming, _ooh_ing at the cub's prowess. Subordinate Authority execs began to show up and take seats, a handful of the privileged who had been invited to see the performance. They muttered approval of Pakka's agility, but stifled it when they saw their boss's deadly look of discontent.

Hirken thumbed his belt unit. A voice answered instantly. "Have the Mark X readied at once." He ignored the crisp acknowledgment from the duty tech, eyed the waiting Bollux, and turned his attention back to the acrobatics. Authority Viceprex Hirken could be very, very patient when he wished, but wasn't in the mood now.

 IX

RIDING down in the elevator, Han concentrated furiously on his predicament.

He'd led the others into this jam thinking that, if nothing else, he'd at least get an idea of what he was up against. At worst, he'd thought, they'd be told they weren't welcome. But this was an unanticipated twist.

That Bollux was committed to a match against a killer robot of some sort shouldn't bother him, Han reminded himself. Bollux was, after all, only a 'droid. It wasn't as if a living entity would die. Han had to keep repeating that because he was having a hard time selling it to himself. Anyway, he had no intention of giving Viceprex Hirken the enjoyment of seeing the superannuated 'droid taken apart.

Times like this, he wished he were the slow, careful type. But his style was the product of Han himself, defying consequences, jumping in with both feet, heedless of what he might land in. His plan, as revised in the elevator, was to do all the scouting he could. If nothing more could be accomplished, he and the others would have to wing it, withdraw from the performance and, it was to be hoped, Stars' End, on the plea that Bollux was irreparable.

He watched floor numbers flash and kept himself

from asking questions of the tech supervisor beside him. Any outsider, particularly an entertainer, would be scrupulously uncurious about an Authority installation. For Han to be otherwise would be a matter causing instant suspicion.

A few other passengers entered and left the car. Only one was an exec; all the rest were Espos and techs. Han looked them over for keys, restraint-binders, or anything else that might indicate detention-block guard duties, but saw nothing. Again he noticed that the tower seemed very lightly manned, contrary to what he'd expect if there really was a prison here.

He followed the tech supervisor out of the elevator, alighting at the general maintenance section, nearly back at ground level. Only a few techs were there, moving among gleaming machinery and dangling hoisting gear. Disassembled 'droids, robo-haulers, and other light equipment, as well as commo and computer apparatus, were to be seen everywhere.

He resettled Max's carrying strap at his shoulder. "Do you guys have a circuit scanner?"

The tech led him to a side room with rows of booths, all of them vacant. Han set Max on a podium in one of them and lowered a scanner hood, hoping the tech would go off and take care of his normal duties. But the man remained there, and so Han found himself staring into the computer-probe's labyrinthine interior.

The tech, watching over his shoulder, commented, "Hey, that looks like a lot more than just an auxiliary component."

"It's something I worked up, pretty sophisticated," Han said. "By the way, the Viceprex said when I'm done here I could take it up to your central computer section to recalibrate it. That's one level down, right?"

The supervisor was frowning now, trying for a better look at Blue Max's guts. "No, computers are two levels up. But they won't let you in unless Hirken verifies it. You're not cleared, and you can't go into a restricted area if you're unbadged." He leaned closer to the scanner. "Listen, that really looks like some kind of computer module to me."

Han chuckled casually. "Here, look for yourself."

He stepped aside. The tech supervisor moved closer to the scanner, reaching down to work its focus controls. Then his own focus went completely dark.

Han, rubbing the edge of his hand, stood over the unconscious tech and looked around for a place to stow him. He had noticed a supply closet at the end of the scanner room. Han fastened the man's hands behind him with his own belt, gagged him with a dust cover off a scanner, and lugged the limp form into the closet. He paused to take the man's security badge, then closed the door.

He went back to the little computer-probe. "All right, Max; perk up."

Blue Max's photoreceptor lit up. Han removed his own sash and stripped the gaudy homemade medals and braid off his outfit. He yanked the epaulets and piping away, too, and what remained was a black body suit, a fair approximation of a tech's uniform. He placed the supervisor's security badge prominently on his chest, took Max up again, and set out. Of course, if anyone were to stop him or compare the miniature holoshot on his badge to his real face, he'd be tubed. But he was counting on his own luck, a convincing briskness of stride, and an air of purpose.

He went up two levels without mishap. Three Espos lounging in the guard booth near the elevator bank waved him on, seeing he was badged. He fought the impulse to smile. Stars' End was probably an uneventful tour of duty; no wonder the guards had gotten lax. After all, what could possibly happen here?

At the amphitheater, Pakka's amazing deftness hadn't even drawn an approving look from Viceprex Hirken. The cub had been using a hoop while rolling a balance-ball with his feet, doing flips.

"Enough of this," Hirken proclaimed, his well-tended hand flying up. Pakka stopped, glaring at the Viceprex. "Isn't that incompetent Marksman back yet?" The other execs, conferring among themselves, managed to reach a group decision that Han was still gone. Hirken's breath rasped.

He pointed to Atuarre. "Very well, Madam, you may dance. But be brief, and if your sharpshooting gaffer isn't back soon, I may dispense with him altogether."

Pakka had removed his props from the arena floor. Now Atuarre handed him the small whistle-flute Han had machined up for him. While the cub blew a few practice runs on it, Atuarre slipped on the finger-cymbals Han had fashioned for her and clinked them experimentally. The improvised instruments, even her anklet-chimes, all lacked the musical quality of Trianii authentics, she decided. But they would suffice, and might even convince the onlookers that they were seeing the real thing.

Pakka began playing a traditional air. Atuarre moved out onto the arena floor, following the music with a sinuous ease no human performer could quite match. Her streamers blew behind her, many-colored fans flickering from arms and legs, forehead and throat, as her finger-cymbals sounded and her anklets rang, precisely as they should.

Some of the preoccupation left Hirken's face and the faces of the other onlookers. Trianni ritual dancing had often been touted as a primitive, uninhibited art, but the truth was that it was high artistry. Its forms were ancient, exacting, demanding all a dancer's concentration. It required perfectionism, and a deep love of the dance itself. In spite of themselves, Hirken, his subordinates, and his wife were drawn into Atuarre's spinning, stalking, pouncing dance. And as she performed, she wondered how long she could hold her audience, and what would happen if she couldn't hold them long enough.

Han, having found a computer terminal in an unoccupied room, set Max down next to it. While Max extended his adapter and entered the system, Han took a cautious look in the hall and closed the door.

He drew up a workstool by a readout screen. "You in, kid?"

"Just about, Captain. The techniques Rekkon taught me work here, too. There!" The screen lit up, flooded with symbols, diagrams, computer models, and columns of data.

"Way to go, Max. Now spot up the holding pens, or cells, or detention levels or whatever."

Blue Max flashed layout after layout on the screen, while his search moved many times faster, skimming huge amounts of data; this was the sort of thing he'd been built for. But at last he admitted, "I can't, Captain."

"What d'you mean, can't? They're here, they've gotta be. Look again, you little moron!"

"There're no cells," Max answered indignantly. "If there were, I'd have seen them. The only living arrangements in the whole base are the employees' housing, the Espo barracks, and the exec suites, all on the other side of the complex—and Hirken's apartments here in the tower."

"All right," Han ordered, "put a floor plan of this joint up, level by level, on the screen, starting with Hirken's amusement park."

A floor plan of the dome, complete with the garden and amphitheater, lit the readout. The next two levels below it proved to be filled with the Viceprex's ostentatious personal quarters. The one after that confused Han. "Max, what're those subdivisions? Offices?"

"It doesn't say here," the computer answered. "The property books list medical equipment, holo-recording gear, surgical servos, operating tables, things like that."

A thought struck Han. "Max, what's Hirken's title? His official corporate job-slot, I mean."

"Vice-President in charge of Corporate Security, it says."

Han nodded grimly. "Keep digging; we're in the right place. That's no clinic up there, it's an interrogation center, probably Hirken's idea of a rec room. What's on the next floor down?"

"Nothing for humans. The next level is three floors high, Captain. Just heavy machinery; there's an industrial-capacity power hookup there, and an air lock. See, here's the floor plan and a power-routing schematic."

Max showed it. Han leaned closer to the screen, studying the myriad lines. One, marked in a different color and located near the elevators, attracted his attention. He asked the computer what it was.

"It's a security viewer, Captain. There's a surveillance system in parts of the tower. I'll patch in."

The screen flickered, then resolved into the brightness of a visual image. Han stared. He'd found the lost ones.

The room was filled, stack upon stack, with stasis booths. Inside each, a prisoner was frozen in time, stopped between one instant and the next by the booth's level-entropy field. That explained why there were no prisoner facilities, no arrangements for handling crowds of captive entities, and only a minimal guard complement on duty. Hirken had all his victims suspended in time; they'd require little in the way of formal accommodations. The Security Viceprex need take prisoners out only when he chose to question them, then pop them back into stasis when he was done. So he robbed his prisoners of their very lives, taking away every part of their existence except interrogation.

"There must be thousands of them," Han breathed. "Hirken can move them in and out of that air lock like freight. Power consumption up there must be terrific. Max, where's their plant?"

"We're sitting on it," Max answered, though that anthropomorphism couldn't really apply to him. He filled the screen with a basic diagram of the tower. Han whistled softly. Beneath Stars' End was a power-generating plant large enough to service a battle fortress, or a capital-class warship.

"And here are the primary defense designs," Max added. There were force fields on all sides of the tower, and one overhead, ready to spring into existence instantly. Stars' End itself was, as Han had already noticed, made of enhanced-bonding armor plate. According to specs, it was equipped with an anticoncussion field as well, so that no amount of high explosives could damage its occupants. The Authority had spared no expense to make its security arrangements complete.

But that helped only if the enemy were outside, and Han was as inside as he could get. "Is there a prisoner roster?"

"Got it! They had it filed: *Transient Persons*."

Han swore under his breath at bureaucratic euphemisms. "Okay, is Chewie's name on it?"

There was the briefest of pauses. "No, Captain. But I found Atuarre's mate! And Jessa's father!" He flashed two more images on the screen, arrest mugshots. Atuarre's mate's coloring was redder than hers, it turned out, and Doc's grizzled features hadn't changed. "And here's Rekkon's nephew," Max added. The mug was of a young black face with broad, strong lines that promised a resemblance to the boy's uncle.

"Jackpot!" Max squealed a moment later, a very uncomputerish exclamation. Chewbacca's big hairy face flashed on the readout. He hadn't been in a very good mood for the mugshot; he was disheveled, but his snarl promised death to the photographer. The Wookiee's eyes looked glassy, and Han assumed that the Espos had tranquilized him as soon as they'd taken him.

"Is he okay?" Han demanded. Max put up the arrest record. No, Chewbacca hadn't been badly injured, but three officers had been killed in apprehending him, the forms said. He hadn't given a name, which explained why it had been difficult for Max to locate him. The list of charges nearly ran off the screen, with a final, ominous, handwritten notation at the bottom listing time of scheduled interrogation. Han glanced at a wall clock; it was no more than hours before Chewbacca was due to enter Viceprex Hirken's torture mill.

"Max, we're up against it. We have to do something

right now; I'm not going to let them take Chewie's mind apart. Can we deactivate defensive systems?"

The computer replied: "Sorry, Captain. All the primaries are controlled through that belt unit Hirken carries."

"What about secondaries?"

Max sounded dubious. "I can get to the standby, but how will you deactivate the Viceprex's belt unit?"

"I dunno; how's he wired up? There must be ancillary equipment; the damn box is too small to be self-contained and still control this whole tower."

Max gave the answer. Receptor circuitry ran through Stars' End, built into the walls on each level.

"Show me the top-level circuitry diagrams." Han studied them carefully, memorizing points of reference —doors, elevators, and support girders.

"Okay, Max, now I want you to cut into the secondary control systems and rearrange power-flow priorities. When the secondaries cut in, I want that umbrella shield, the deflector directly overhead, to start load-shedding its power back to the plant, but I want you to prejudice the systems' safeguards, so that they notice the deflector droppage but not the feedback."

"Captain Solo, that'll start an overload spiral. You could blow the whole tower up."

"Only if I get to Hirken's primaries," Han said, half to himself, half to Max. "Get crackin'."

High above, Viceprex Hirken had realized that he was being played for a fool.

As fascinated as he'd been by Atuarre's dance, he'd recognized in a fundamental, ever-suspicious part of his mind that he was being diverted. What he desired was to see mechanized combat. This dance artistry, though pretty enough, was no substitute.

He stood, fingering a button on his belt unit. Lights came up, and Pakka stopped playing. Atuarre looked around her, as if awakening from a dream. "What—"

"Enough of this," Hirken decreed. Uul-Rha-Shan, his reptilian gunman, stood at his side, hoping for the order to slay. But instead, Hirken said, "I've seen enough, Trianii. You're clearly stalling. You think me an imbecile?" Then he motioned to Bollux. "You ridiculous excuses for entertainers brought this obsolete 'droid to me purely as a fraud, never planning to give me value for my money. You'd hoped to plead mechanical failure and get me to reimburse you for your trip, or even reward you for your efforts. Isn't that so?"

Her quiet "No, Viceprex" was ignored.

Hirken was not convinced. "Prepare that 'droid for combat, and bring out my Mark X," he ordered the techs and Espos around him.

Atuarre drew herself up, enraged, and afraid for Bollux. But she could see Hirken was adamant, and she had her cub to think of. Furthermore she could do Han and her mate little good here. "With your permission, Excellency, I will return to my ship." Onboard the *Falcon,* at least, more options would be available.

Hirken waved her away, preoccupied with his Executioner, laughing his humorless laugh. "Go, go. And if you see that worthless liar of a Marksman of yours, you'd be wise to take him with you. And don't think I won't lodge a complaint. I'll have your Guild membership revoked."

She glanced to where Bollux was being ushered down to the arena, helpless to aid him. "Lord Hirken, surely this is illegal. That is our 'droid—"

"Brought here to defraud me," he finished for her, "but I'll have my value from it. Now leave, if you're going to, or watch if you wish." He wagged a finger, and an Espo sergeant barked an order. Tall, stern guards fell in, one to either side of the two Trianii.

Atuarre couldn't restrain her hiss. She grabbed Pakka's paw and stormed toward the elevator, the cub bouncing along behind. Uul-Rha-Shan's dry laugh was like a stab of hatred.

Down in the computer center, the readout screen, which had been showing a small part of the modifica-

145

tion Blue Max was making, went blank for a moment.

"Max? You all right?" Han asked worriedly.

"Captain Solo, they're activating that combat machine, the Mark X. They're putting it in with Bollux!" Even as the computer-probe spoke, the rapid-fire images of the Mark-X Executioner's engineering details replaced one another on the screen. Max's voice was filled with alarm. "The Mark X's controls and power are independent of this system; I can't touch it! Captain, we have to get back upstairs right now. Bollux needs me!"

"What about Atuarre?"

"They're summoning an elevator and notifying security that she's leaving. We've got to get up there!"

Han was shaking his head, unmindful that Max's photoreceptor was off. "Sorry, Max, there're too many other things I need to do here. Besides, we couldn't help Bollux now."

The readout went blank and the photoreceptor came on. Blue Max's voice trembled. "Captain Solo, I'm not doing anything else for you until you take me to Bollux. I *can* help him."

Han struck the probe, not gently, with the heel of his hand. "Get back to work, Max. I'm serious." For answer, Max withdrew his adapter from the network. Han, infuriated, snatched the little computer up and held it high overhead.

"Do what I told you, or I'll leave you here in pieces!"

Max's reply was somber. "Go ahead, then, Captain. Bollux would do whatever he had to if I were in trouble."

Han paused in the midst of dashing the computer to the floor. It occurred to him that Max's concern for his friend was no different from Han's own for Chewbacca. He lowered the probe, looking at it as if for the first time. "I'll be damned. You sure you can help Bollux?"

"Just get me there, Captain; you'll see!"

"I hope. Which car was going to the dome?"

Max told him, and he set out for the elevators at

once, slinging the probe over his shoulder. When he got there, he removed the security badge and punched for a downward ride. The wrong car stopped; he let it wait and go on, and punched the descent button again.

He lucked out. The car containing Atuarre, Pakka, and their two guards had stopped a number of times on its way down. She saw Han and pulled her cub off the car with her. The Espos had to hurry to avoid being left behind.

Han took the two Trianii aside a pace or two, but the Espos made it plain that they were keeping an eye on all three.

"We were going to the ship," Atuarre told him in low tones. "I didn't know what else to do. Solo-Captain, Hirken is putting Bollux in with that Executioner machine of his!"

"I know. Max has some kind of angle on that." He saw one of the Espos speaking on a com-link. "Listen, the lost ones are here, thousands of 'em. Max rigged the tower; Hirken'll have to let everybody go if he wants to keep breathing. Go get the ship ready. If I can just get my hands on a blaster, the fix is in, sister."

"Captain, I meant to tell you," Max interrupted. "I was rechecking the figures. I think you should know—"

"Not now, Max!" Han pulled Atuarre and Pakka back toward the elevator, hitting both the up and the down buttons. One of the Espos fell in with the Trianii again, but the other stationed himself with Han, explaining, "The Viceprex says it's all right for you to come up. You can take home what's left of your 'droid after the fight."

The techs and Espos hurried Bollux down into the arena as the transparisteel slabs raised from their hidden slots in the floor. Hirken knew now that this was no gladiator 'droid, and so gave the command that Bollux be equipped with a blast shield, to make things more interesting. The shield, an oblong of dura-armor plate fitted with grips, weighed down the old 'droid's long arm as he tried to adjust to what was happening.

Bollux knew he would never escape so many armed men. He had known many humans in his long years of function and could recognize hatred by now. That was what he saw on the Viceprex's face. But Bollux had come through a number of seemingly terminal situations and had no intention of being demolished now if he could avoid it.

A door panel slid up in the far wall forming one arc of the arena. There was a squeal of drive wheels, the rattling of treads. The Mark-X Executioner rolled out into the light.

It was half again as tall as Bollux and far broader, though it moved on two thick caterpillar tracks instead of legs. From the treads and support housing rose a thick trunk, armored in gray alloy plate. The Executioner's many arms were folded close to it now, inactive, each one furnished with a different weapon.

Bollux employed a trick he had learned from one of his first human owners, and simply omitted from computations the logical conclusion that his destruction was now a high order of probability. Among humans, he knew, this tactic was called ignoring certain death. Bollux thought of it as excluding counterproductive data. He'd been doing it for a long time now, which was why he was still functional.

The Executioner's cranial turret swung, its sensors locking in on the 'droid. The Mark X was the latest word in combat automata, an extremely successful, highly specialized killing machine. It could have zeroed in on the unarmed, general-purpose labor 'droid and vaporized him right then and there, but was, naturally, programmed to give its owner a more enjoyable show than that. The Executioner was also a machine with a purpose.

The Mark X began rolling, moving with quick precision, maneuvering toward Bollux. The 'droid backed away clumsily, contending with the unfamiliar task of holding and manipulating his blast shield. The Executioner circled, studying Bollux from all sides, gauging his reactions, while the 'droid watched from behind his shield.

"Commence!" called Viceprex Hirken through the arena's amplifiers. The Mark X, voice-keyed to him, changed to attack mode. It came directly to bear on Bollux, rushing at him at top speed. The 'droid dodged one way, then another, but his efforts were all anticipated by the Executioner. It compensated for his every move, rumbling to crush him under its treads.

"Cancel!" rasped Hirken over the amplifiers. The Mark X stopped just short of Bollux, allowing the old 'droid to totter awkwardly back from it.

"Resume!" ordered the Viceprex. The Executioner cranked into motion again, selecting another destructive option from its arsenal. Servos hummed and a weapon arm came up, its end supporting a flame projector. Bollux saw it and brought his shield up just in time.

A gush of fire arced from the nozzle of the flame gun, splashing against the walls of the arena, throwing a burning stream across Bollux's shield. The Mark X brought the nozzle of its weapon back for another pass at low angle, to cut the 'droid's legs out from under him. Bollux barely managed to crash clumsily to his knees and ground his shield before flame washed across it, making puddles of fire on the floor around him. The Mark X was rolling again, preparing for a clearer shot, when Hirken canceled that mode, too.

Bollux struggled to his feet, using the shield for leverage. He could feel his internal mechanisms overheating, his bearings especially. His gyro-balance circuitry hadn't been built with this sort of constant punishment in mind.

Then the Mark X was coming in again. Bollux ignored the inevitable, making his sluggish parts respond, moving with some mechanical equivalent of pain, but still functional.

Han came out of the elevator at a run. The Espos there, aware that the Viceprex wished him to see the spectacle, let him pass.

He skidded to a stop at the top row of the little amphitheater. Hirken was seated below with his wife and subordinates, cheering their champion and laughing at the ludicrous Bollux as the Executioner raised another weapon arm. This one was provided with a bracket of flechette-missile pods.

Bollux saw it, too, and used a trick, or, as he thought of it, a last variable. Crouching, still holding his shield, he loosed the heavy-duty suspension in his legs and jumped out of the Mark X's cross hairs like some giant red insect. Miniature missiles exploded against the clear arena walls in a cloud, filling the amphitheater with crashing eruptions in spite of the sound-suppression system out in the seating area.

Hirken and his people roared their frustration. Han flung himself down the steps to the arena, three at a time. Bollux had landed badly; the strain on his mechanisms was becoming insuperable. The Viceprex changed his combat-automaton's programming once more.

The Executioner retracted its missile-arm. Articulated catch-cables extended from ports in its sides, like metallic tentacles, and two circular saws swung out, their arms locking into position. The sawblades spun, creating a peculiar sound, the molecules of their cutting edges vibrating in a way that would shear through metal as easily as through air. The Mark X moved toward Bollux, its cables weaving, for a terminal embrace.

Hirken spied Han reaching the arena's edge. "Fraud! Now, watch a true combat-automaton at work!" He shook with gruesome laughter, all the affected charms of corporate board rooms stripped from him now. His wife and subordinates followed suit dutifully.

Han ignored them and held up the computer. "Max, tell him!" Blue Max sent burst-signals at top volume, concentrated pulses of information. Bollux turned his red photoreceptors to home in on the probe. He listened for a moment, then returned his attention to the onrushing Mark X. Han, knowing it was crazy, still found himself holding his breath.

As the Executioner bore down on him, Bollux made no move to avoid it or raise his shield. The Executioner recognized that as only logical. The 'droid had no hope. Questing catch-cables spread wide to seize Bollux; circular saws swung close.

Bollux hefted his shield and threw it at the Mark X. Cables and cutters changed course; the shield was easily intercepted, caught, and sliced to pieces. But in the moment's reprieve, Bollux had thrown himself, stiffly—with a huge metallic *bong*—down between the crushing treads of the Executioner.

The combat-automaton ground to a halt, but not in time. Bollux, lying beneath it, fastened one hand to its undercarriage and locked his servo-grip there. The other hand reached in among the components of the Mark X, ripping at its cooling circuitry.

The Executioner emitted an electronic scream. If it had sat there and pondered for an age, the killing machine would still never have considered the possibility that a general-labor 'droid could have learned how to do the irrational.

The Mark X broke into motion, rolling this way and that, randomly. It had no way to get at Bollux, who clung beneath it. No one had ever programmed the Executioner to shoot at itself, or cut at itself, or to crush something it couldn't reach. Bollux was in the single safe place in the entire arena.

The Mark X's internal temperature began rising at once; the killing machine produced enormous amounts of heat.

Hirken was on his feet now, screaming: *"Cancel! Cancel!* Executioner, I order you to *cancel!"* Techs began running around, bumping into one another, but the Mark X was no longer receiving orders. Its complicated voice-keyed command circuitry had been among the first things to go out of whack. Now it charged aimlessly around the arena, discharging blasters, flame guns, and missile pods at random, threatening to overload the noise-suppression system.

The arena's transparisteel walls became a window into an inferno as the Executioner roamed, its trunk rotating, its weapons blazing, its malfunctioning guidance system seeking an enemy that it could confront. It was hit by shrapnel from its own missiles. Smoke and fire could be seen pouring from its ventilators. Bollux hung on to the Mark X's undercarriage with both hands now, being dragged back and forth, wondering calmly if his grip would fail.

The Executioner rebounded from one of the arena's walls. Surviving targeting circuits thought the killing machine had found its enemy at last. It backed up, preparing for another charge, its engine revving.

Bollux decided correctly that it was time to part company. He simply let go. The Executioner howled off again, all its remaining attention focused on the unoffending wall. The 'droid began to drag himself, squeaking laboriously, toward the exit.

The Executioner crashed head-on into the arena wall, bouncing back with a mighty concussion. Frustrated, it fired all weapons at close range and was engulfed in the backwash of blaster beams, flechette fragments, and acid spray. Then, as Hirken cried a last *"No-ooo!"*, the Mark X's internal heat reached critical, compounded by external damage.

The Mark-X Executioner, latest word in combat automata, was ruptured open by a spectacular explosion just as Bollux, semiobsolete general-labor 'droid, got his tired chassis out of the arena.

Han knelt by him, pounding the old 'droid on the back while Blue Max somehow produced a cheer from his vocoder. The pilot threw his head back and laughed, forgetting everything else in the absurdity of the moment.

"Give me a minute, please," Bollux begged, his drawl even slower now. "I must try to bring my mechanisms into some sort of order."

"I can help!" Max squeaked. "Link me through to your brain circuits, Bollux, and I'll handle all the bypasses. That'll leave you free to deal with the cyberostasis problems."

Bollux opened his plastron. "Captain, if you'd be so kind?" Han put the little computer back into place.

"Touching, whoever you are," said a smooth, dry voice behind Han, "but pointless. We'll pick them both apart for the information we want. What happened to all your pretty braid and medals, by the way?"

Han turned and stood fast. Uul-Rha-Shan was waiting there, gun in hand. Han's holstered blaster hung over the reptilian gunman's shoulder.

Hirken came up behind Uul-Rha-Shan, followed by the major and the other Espos, his execs, and his wife, all the trappings of his corporate importance. The air was filled with the smell of charred circuitry and molten metal, all that remained of the precious Mark X. Hirken's face held inexpressible rage.

He pointed a quivering finger at Han. "I should've known you're part of the conspiracy! Trianii, 'droids, the Entertainers' Guild—they're all in on it. No one on the Board will be able to deny it now; this conspiracy against the Authority and against me personally involves *everyone!*"

Han shook his head, amazed. Hirken was sweating, bellowing, with a maniacal look on his face. "I don't know your real name, Marksman, but you've come to the end of this plot. What I need to know, I'll dig out of your 'droid, and the Trianii. But since you've spoiled my entertainment, you'll make up for it."

He went with the rest of his entourage and stood just inside the arena, safe behind the transparisteel slabs. Uul-Rha-Shan took Han's gunbelt from his shoulder and held it out to him. "Come, trick shooter. Let's see if you have any tricks left."

Han moved warily and collected the belt. He checked his holstered blaster by eye, and saw that it had been drained of all but a microcharge, not enough to damage the primary-control circuitry. His gaze went to Hirken, who stood gloating behind invulnerable transparisteel. The belt control unit was out of the question. Han climbed the amphitheater stairs slowly, buckling the gunbelt around his hips, tying down the holster.

Uul-Rha-Shan came after, returning his disrupter to its forearm holster. The two stepped out onto the open area overlooking the arena; the gathered Authority officials looked up at them.

It had been a good try, Han told himself, just a touch shy of success. But now Hirken meant to see him dead, and Chewbacca and Atuarre and Pakka in his interrogation chambers. The Viceprex held all the cards but one. Han made up his mind on the spot that if he was going to die anyway, he'd take all these warped minds of Corporate Security with him.

He went, carefully, and stood by the wall, unsnapping the retaining strap of his holster. His opponent, squared off a few paces away, wasn't through taunting.

"Uul-Rha-Shan likes to know whom he kills. Who are you, imposter?"

Drawing himself up, Han let his hands dangle loosely at his sides, fingers working. "Solo. Han Solo."

The reptile registered surprise. "I have heard your name, Solo. You are, at least, worthy of the killing."

Han's mouth tugged, amused. "Think you can bring it off, lizard?"

Uul-Rha-Shan hissed anger. Han cleared his mind of everything but what lay before him.

"Farewell, Solo," Uul-Rha-Shan bade him, tensing.

Han moved with a dipping motion of the right shoulder, a half turn, all done with the blinding abruptness of the gunfighter. But his hand never closed on the grip of his blaster.

Instead, feigning his draw, he hurled himself out on the floor. As he fell, he felt Uul-Rha-Shan's disrupter beam lash over him, striking the wall. It set off a belching explosion that caught the reptile full in the face, flinging him backward. His shot had blown apart the ancillary circuitry for Hirken's belt unit, freeing swirls of energy. Secondary explosions told of the destruction of power-management routers.

Han had hit the floor rolling, surviving the blast with little more than singed hair. His blaster was in his hand now, the cautionary pulser in its grip tingling his palm in silent, invisible warning that the gun was nearly empty. As if he needed to be reminded. Uul-Rha-Shan, somewhere in the din and smoke, was shrilling, "Solo-ooo!" in furious challenge. Han couldn't pick him out.

A far-off vibration reached him, the overload spiral he'd had Blue Max build into the secondary defense program. Now that the primaries had been damaged and Hirken's belt unit circumvented, the power-rerouting had taken over. Won't be long now, he told himself.

Everyone in Stars' End suddenly felt as if he were being immersed in thick mud, as the weight of a planet seemed to be pressing down. The anticoncussion field —Han had forgotten about it, but it didn't matter.

Then, with an explosion beyond words, the power plant blew.

 X

ATUARRE restrained herself from running back through the maze of tunnel-tubes, conscious of the Espo guard at her heels. Han's desperate plan left her so much room for doubt. What would happen if the bluff failed? But on that thought she corrected herself at once—Solo-Captain was not bluffing, and was more than capable of taking all his enemies with him in an act of awesome revenge.

But she approved of the gamble. This might be Stars' End's only vulnerable moment. Even so, she took her longest strides now, dragging a stumbling Pakka along breakneck-quick.

They passed into the final junction station, the one nearest the *Falcon*. A tech lounged on duty behind his console. The Espo's com-link signaled for attention, and Atuarre heard the crackled order, relayed from Hirken through the Espo major, as clearly as did her escort himself. The two Trianii were to be brought back to the tower. She wondered if that meant Han had successfully intervened in Bollux's combat.

But Atuarre had no intention of going back now; Solo-Captain specifically wanted her onboard the *Millennium Falcon*. She tried her most reasonable tone. "Officer, I have to pick up a very important item on my ship, then we can return. Please? It's very vital; that's why I was given clearance to go in the first place."

The Espo wasn't paying heed. He drew his side arm. "Orders say *at once*. Move it!"

The attention of the duty tech was aroused now, but the guard was the immediate danger. Atuarre held Pakka's paw high, so that his toes barely touched the floor, showing him to the guard. "You see, I was also told to leave my cub onboard ship. His presence displeased the Viceprex." She felt Pakka's short, elastic muscles tighten.

The Espo opened his mouth to reply, and she whipped the cub up. Pakka took snapping momentum from the launch, and both of the Trianii split the air with predatory howls, astounding the Authority men.

Pakka's dropkick caught the astonished Espo in the face and throat. Atuarre, coming in behind her cub, threw herself on the man's arm, prying his hand loose from his blaster. The Trianii bore their antagonist over backward, the cub with arms and legs and tail wrapped around the Espo's head and neck, Atuarre wrenching the blaster free.

She heard a scuffle of sound behind her. Whirling, she saw the duty tech half standing from his chair behind the console. His left forefinger was stabbing some button on his board, hard. She assumed it to be an alarm, but the tech's right hand was bringing up a blaster, and that was first on the agenda. She fired with the dispatch of a Trianii Ranger. The brief red flash of the blaster knocked the tech off his feet, backward, overturning his chair.

The Espo, bleeding from his wounds, threw Pakka off and charged at Atuarre, hands clutching for her. She fired again, the red bolt lighting the junction station. The Espo buckled and lay still. She could hear alarms jangling through the tunnel-tube layout.

Atuarre was about to go to the junction station console, to disconnect the tunnel-tubes and cut off pursuit, when the station jolted on its treads, as if the surface of Mytus VII had surged up under it. She and Pakka were bounced in the air like toys by the tremors of an explosion of incredible force.

Atuarre picked herself up dazedly and staggered to one of the thick exterior observation ports. She couldn't see the tower. Instead, a column of incandescent fire had sprung up where Stars' End had stood. It seemed impossibly thin and high, reaching far up into the vacuous sky of Mytus VII.

Then she realized that the force of the explosion had been contained by deflector-shield generators around the tower. The pillar of destruction began to dissipate, but she could see nothing of Stars' End, not a fragment. She couldn't believe that even an exploding power plant could utterly vaporize the nearly impregnable tower.

Then, on some impulse, she looked up, beyond the tip of the explosion's flare. High above Mytus VII she saw the wink of the small distant sun off enhanced-bonding armor plate.

"Oh, Solo-Captain," she breathed, understanding what had happened, "you *madman!*"

She pushed herself away from the port unsteadily and assessed her situation. She must move without hesitation. She raced to the console, found separator switches, and matching them with indicators over the junction station's tunnel-tubes, worked the three not connected to the *Falcon*. The tubes disengaged, their lengths contracting back toward the junction, pleating in on themselves.

Then she brought the junction station's self-propulsion unit to life, setting its treads in motion, steering it toward the *Millennium Falcon,* gathering in the intervening tube length as she went.

She chilled the discord in her mind with the discipline expected of a Trianii Ranger, and a plan began to form. One minute later, the *Millennium Falcon* raised from Mytus VII.

Atuarre, at the controls with Pakka perched in the copilot's chair, scanned the base. She knew the personnel must be coping desperately with pressure droppages and air leaks through their ruptured systems. But the armed Espo assault ship had already boosted clear of the base; she could see its engine glowing as it climbed rapidly in the distance. That someone had comprehended what had happened and responded so quickly gave her one more worry. No more Authority ships must be allowed to lift off.

She guided the starship in a low pass at the line of smaller Authority vessels. The *Falcon*'s guns spoke again and again in a close strafing run. The parked, pilotless ships burst and flared one after another, yielding secondary explosions. Of the half-dozen craft there, none escaped damage. She swooped past the deep crater where Stars' End had once stood.

She opened the main drive, screaming off after the departed Espo assault craft. She kept all shields angled aft, but there was only sporadic, inaccurate turbolaser cannon fire. The personnel at the base were too busy trying to keep the breath of life from bleeding off into the vacuum. That was one advantage, a small help to her in what seemed like a hopeless task.

Stars' End's anticoncussion field must very nearly have overloaded, Han thought; for the first seconds after the power plant blew, stupendous forces had been exerted on the tower and everything in it. But the immobilizing effect began to recede as the systems adjusted.

Smoke and heat from both the ruined Executioner and the now-defunct primary-control ancillaries rolled and drifted through the dome, choking and blinding.

There was a universal rush of indistinct bodies for the elevators. Han could hear Hirken yelling for order as the Espo major bellowed commands and the Viceprex's wife and others shrilled in panic.

Han skirted the mob headed for the elevators, wading through the anticoncussion field and the drifting smoke. Like all standbys, the anticoncussion field fed off emergency power inside Stars' End. The tower's reserves would be limited. Han grinned in the murk and confusion; the Espos were in for a surprise.

He made his way down the steps of the amphitheater, groping along, coughing and hoping he wasn't being poisoned by burned insulation and molten circuitry. His toe hit something. He recognized Viceprex Hirken's discarded belt unit, kicked it aside, and went on. He located Bollux when he stumbled over the 'droid's foot.

"Captain, sir!" Bollux hailed. "We'd thought you'd quite left, sir."

"We're bowing out now; can you make it?"

"I'm stabilized. Max improvised a direct linkup between himself and me."

Blue Max's voice drifted up from Bollux's chest. "Captain, I *tried* to tell you when I rechecked the figures that this might happen."

Han had gotten a hand under the 'droid's arm, helping him to rise to his wobbly legs. "What *did* happen, Max? Not enough power in the plant?" He started moving Bollux off unsteadily through the drifting reek.

"No, there was plenty of power in the plant, but the enhanced-bonding armor plate is a lot stronger than I thought at first. The exterior deflector shields contained the force of the explosion, all except the overhead one, the one that dissolved in the overload. All the force went that way. Us too."

Han stopped. He wished he could see the little computer, not that it would have helped. "Max, are you telling me we blew Stars' End into *orbit?*"

"No, Captain," Max answered darkly. "A high-arc trajectory, maybe, but never an orbit."

Han found himself leaning on Bollux as much as the 'droid was leaning on him. "Oh, my! Why didn't you warn me?"

"I *tried*," Max reminded him sulkily.

Han was in mental overdrive. It made sense: Mytus VII's relatively light specific gravity and lack of atmospheric friction must give it an escape velocity that was only middlin'. Still, if the tower's anticoncussion fields hadn't been on when the large charge had gone off, everybody in Stars' End would've been colloidal slime by now.

"Besides," Max added testily, "isn't this better than being dead? So far?"

Han brightened; there was no arguing with that logic. He shouldered part of Bollux's weight again. "Okay, men; I have a new plan. Forward!" They reeled off again, away from the elevators. "All the elevators will be out; life-support and whatnot will have pre-empted all the reserve power. I saw a utility stairwell in the floor plans, but Hirken and Company will be remembering it pretty soon, too. Shag it."

They rounded the curve of the utility core as Han took his bearings. They were almost to a yellow-painted emergency door when the door snapped open and an Espo jumped out, riot gun in hand. Cupping his hand to his mouth, the man called, "Viceprex Hirken! This way, sir!"

Then he noticed Han and Bollux and swung his weapon to bear. With only a microcharge in the blaster, Han had to make a quick head shot. The Espo dropped.

"Brown nose," Han grunted, still hanging on to the 'droid, stooping to grab the riot gun. He manhandled himself and his burden through the emergency door. A furor of shouting reached him; the others had found the elevators useless, and someone had remembered the stairwell. Han secured the door behind him and fired several sustained bursts at its latching mechanism. The metal began to glow and fuse. It was a durable alloy that would shed its heat again in moments, leaving the latch welded shut. Those remaining on the other side would be able to blast their way through with hand weapons, but it would take precious time.

As he and Han half fell, half ran, down the stairs, Bollux asked, "Where to now, sir?"

"The stasis-booth tiers." They careened around a landing, nearly falling. "Feel that? The artificial gravity's fluctuating. In time the power-management routers will cut off everything but life-support."

"Oh, I see, sir." Bollux said. "The stasis booths you and Max mentioned!"

"Give the 'droid a prize. When those booths start conking out, there're gonna be some pretty cranky prisoners on the loose. The guy who might be able to pull our choobies out of the conflagration is one of them—Doc, Jessa's father."

They made their way down, past Hirken's living quarters and the interrogation levels, encountering no one else in the stairwell. The gravity fluctuations lessened, but footing remained unpredictable. They arrived at another emergency door, and Han opened it manually.

Across a corridor was another door, which had been left open. Through it Han saw a long, wide aisle between high tiers of stasis booths like stacked, upright coffins. The lowest rows of booths were already darkened, empty, the highest still in operation. Booths in the middle two rows flickered.

But down in the aisles a line of six guards wavered before a mass of humans and nonhumans. The released prisoners, members of dozens of species, growled and roared their hostility. Fists, tentacles, claws, and paws shook angrily in the air. The Espos, waving their riot guns and advancing, tried to contain the break without firing, afraid they might be overwhelmed if they opened up.

A tall, demonish-looking being broke from the mob and launched himself at the Espos, his face splitting with mad laughter, hands grasping. A burst from a riot gun brought him down in a groaning heap. The prisoners' hesitation disappeared; they advanced on the

Espos in unison. What did they have to fear from death, compared with life in the interrogation chambers?

Han pushed Bollux aside, knelt behind the emergency-door frame, and cut loose at the guards. Two of them fell before they realized they were taking fire from their rear. One turned, then another, to exchange shots, while their fellows tried to hold back the seething prisoners.

Red darts of light crisscrossed. Smoke from charred metal rose from the doorframe with the ozone of blaster fire. The smell of burned flesh was in the air. The unnerved guards' bolts zipped through the open emergency door or hit the wall, but failed to find their target. Han, kneeling to make himself as small a mark as possible, winced and flinched from the intense counterfire and cursed his own riot gun's poor sighting characteristics.

He finally nailed one of the two Espos shooting at him. The other dropped to the floor to avoid being hit. Han, seeing that, used an old trick. Reaching through the doorframe, he placed his weapon flat on its side on the floor, triggering frantically. The shots, aligned directly along the plane of the floor, found the prone Espo and silenced him in seconds.

The remaining guards broke. One let his piece fall and raised his hands, but it did him no good; the mob poured over and around him like an avalanche, burying him in murderous human and alien forms. The other Espo, trapped between Han's sniping and the prisoners, started scaling one of the ladders connecting the catwalks along the tiers of stasis booths.

Partway up, the guard paused and shot those who had tried to follow him. Han's shots, at the wrong angle, missed. Han gathered up Bollux, headed for the tier room.

The last Espo's gunfire had made the prisoners draw back as he climbed for the third catwalk. From out of the pack of prisoners, three shaggy, simian creatures swarmed up after him, disdaining ladders, swinging up arm over long arm along the tiers' outerworks. They overtook the Espo in moments.

He hung from the rungs long enough to shoot one of the simians. It fell with an eerie caw. The other ape-things drew even with the Espo, one on either side. As he tried to fire again, his weapon was snatched from his hand and dropped to those below. The yowling guard was then caught up by both his arms, swung, and hurled with incredible strength straight upward. He slammed against the ceiling above the highest row of booths and fell to the floor in a windmilling of arms and legs, with an ugly sound of impact.

Han, setting Bollux aside, ran to join the milling prisoners. Overhead, more and more of the stasis booths were being shut down to power the overtaxed life-support systems, yielding inhabitants of many planets. Now that the immediate challenge of the guards had been eliminated, the recent escapees were at a loss. Many of them had been killed or wounded by the guards' fire, and many others were dead or dying, unwounded, because their physiologies weren't compatible with Stars' End's atmosphere and they hadn't entered stasis with their life-support equipment. Voices overbore one another: "Hey, where are—" "The gravity's funny! What's happ—" "What place is this?"

Han, yelling and waving, got their attention. "Grab those guns and take up positions in the stairwell! Espos will be finding their way here in a minute!" He spotted a man in the uniform of a planetary constabulary, probably a bothersome official the Authority had decided to put on ice. Han pointed to him. "Get them organized and set up defenses, or you'll all find yourself back in stasis!"

Han turned, heading for the corridor. As he passed the 'droid, he told him, "Wait here, Bollux; I've got to find Doc and Chewie."

As the prisoners scrambled for the fallen Espos' weapons, Han dashed into the connecting corridor, swung right, and headed for the next tier block. But as he closed on the next door, it snapped open, unlocked from the inside. Three Espos crowded, elbows and hips, each trying to be the first to get out of the tier block, as a pandemonium of fighting and shooting echoed from the room behind them.

The guards made it only halfway through the door. There was a deafening roar, and a familiar pair of long hairy arms reached out to gather all three of them back into the fray.

"Yo, there you are now," Han called happily. "Chewie!"

The Wookiee had finished draping the guards' limp forms over a nearby handrail. He saw his friend and hooted ecstatically. Han, his protestations ignored, was caught up in a comradely embrace that made his ribs creak. Then the artificial gravity waffled for a second and Chewbacca nearly fell. He let Han down.

"If we ever get out of this, partner," Han panted, "let's go settle down on a nice, quiet, stellar delivery route, what d'you say?"

This tier block had been taken with less trouble than the other; apparently fewer guards had been here when its stasis fields began to go. There was the same confusion, though, in a multitude of tongues and sound levels. The Wookiee, jostled into Han, turned with a truly stentorian roar, holding his fists aloft. A space cleared around him instantly. Into the interval of silence Han inserted the order that the prisoners take up what guns they had and join the other defenders.

Then he grabbed Chewbacca's shoulder. "C'mon, Doc's here somewhere, Chewie, and we haven't got long to find him. He's our only chance of coming out of this alive."

The two went on to the next tier block, of which there were five altogether, as Han recalled from the floor plan. They encountered a door already open. Han brought the riot gun up and peered cautiously into the chamber. Its stasis booths were empty, and a disturbing silence hung over all. Han wondered if, perhaps, the Authority hadn't gotten to use this portion

of its prison yet. He stepped into the tier block; Chewbacca followed after.

"Stand where you are!" ordered a voice behind
them. Men and other creatures jumped up from concealment on the catwalks and outerworks, and along
the walls. More appeared from around the bend in
the corridor.

But both Han and his first mate had identified the
voice that had commanded them. "Doc!" Han cried,
though he and the Wookiee prudently held their
places. No use being fried.

The old man, his head wreathed by a white, frizzy
cloud of hair, blinked at them in utter surprise. "Han
Solo! What in the name of the Original Light brings
you here, son? But I suppose that's obvious: two more
inmates, eh?" He faced the others. "This pair's okay."

He trotted over to them. Han was shaking his head,
"No, Doc. Chewie was here. A few of us came to see
what we—"

Doc hushed him. "More important things to get to,
youngster. All these tiers in the first three rooms went
at once; that's how we took the blocks so quickly. The
demands on the systems must've been extraordinary;
and now I notice the gravity's unstable."

Three tier blocks going all at once figured, Han
thought, what with that first giant demand placed on
the anticoncussion fields when the power plant went.
"Uh, yeah, Doc. I meant to mention that. You know
you're in a tower, right? Well, I, I sort of blew it into
space; overloaded the power plant and cut the overhead deflector shield so that—"

Doc clapped a hand over his eyes. "Han, you *imbecile!*"

Han became defensive. "You don't like it? Climb
back into your shipping crate!" He saw he'd made his
point. "No time to argue; there's no way Stars' End
can make it all the way out of Mytus VII's gravity.
We're due for a crash, and I'm not sure how soon.
The only thing that'll save us is that anticoncussion
field, and it's faded. It's up to you to make sure it's
juiced up when we hit."

Doc was staring at Han with his mouth open. "Sonny, energizing an anticoncussion field is *not* like hot-wiring somebody's skyhopper and going for a joyride!"

Han threw his hands up. "Fine; let's just sit and wait to smash ourselves flat. Jessa can always adopt a new father."

That struck home. Doc sighed. "You're right; if it's our one shot, we shall take it. But I don't think much of your taste in jailbreaks." He turned to the others, who had been kept from intruding in the conversation only because of Chewbacca's looming presence. "Pay attention! No time for chatting! Come with me, and do as I say, and we may make it yet; at least I can promise you an end to interrogation."

He elbowed Han. "Blaze of glory, and all that, eh?" Then he started off at the head of a shuffling, loping, hoof-clacking horde, each individual moving on whatever extremities or in whatever fashion was his.

As they went, Han rapidly told Doc the bare bones of the story. The old man interrupted: "This Trianii is onboard the *Millennium Falcon*?"

"Should be, but it won't do us much good; the *Falcon*'s tractors could never hold back this tower from re-entry."

Doc stopped. "I say, did you hear something, boy?"

They all had, the mew and crackle of blaster fire. They broke into a run. For all his apparent age, Doc kept up with the pilot and the Wookiee. They reached the emergency door just as the limp body of a prisoner was passed into the corridor from the stairwell. It was a gangling, saurian creature with a blaster burn in its midsection. From the stairwell came the irregular sounds of a firefight.

"What's going on?" Han shouted, trying to elbow his way through. Chewbacca got in front, shoving and yelping, and opened a way. The prisoner who Han had arbitrarily put in charge appeared on the stairs. "We're holding an upper landing. There are a number of Authority people up there, trying to fight their way down. I put some lookouts on the lower stairs, but nothing's happened down there yet."

"Hirken and his bunch are trying to make their way down because the air locks are located here and on the lowest level. He's hoping for a rescue," Han told them.

Doc and the others looked at him in surprise. He remembered that Stars' End must be largely unknown territory to them. The constabulary officer asked, "Just what's happened?"

"Our time's running out, is what," Han answered. "We have to hold up here and give Doc there a chance to get down to the engineering levels. Take whoever's armed on point; there'll be some resistance down there, but it ought to be light. The rest can follow at a distance."

The expedition down the stairwell began, with Doc hurrying because none of them knew when the tower would hit its apogee and begin its plummeting descent.

Meanwhile, Han and Chewbacca dashed upstairs. Han felt himself breathing hard and understood that life-support systems were beginning to fail. If the oxygen pressure in the tower fell too low, all their efforts would mean nothing.

They joined the defenders holding the second landing above the tier blocks. Blaster beams from above sizzled and crashed against the opposite wall as the remaining armed prisoners here fired quick, unaimed shots around the corner when they could, with little chance of hitting anyone up on the next landing. Several defenders lay dead or injured. As Han topped the stairs, one man edged his weapon around the corner, quickly squeezed off a few shots, and drew back hastily. He spied Han. "What's going on down there?"

Han crouched beside him and was about to ease around the corner for a squint upstairs when a volley of red bolts burned and bit at the floor and walls out in the field of fire. He shrank back.

"Get your bulb down, man," the defender cautioned. "We ran into their point men right here at the turn. We drove them back, but the rest came

167

down. It's a standoff, but they have more weapons."
Then he repeated, "What's going on below?"

"The others are headed for the lower levels, to rig a,
a way out of this. We're here to keep the riffraff out."
He began to sweat, thinking that the tower must surely
be succumbing to the pull of Mytus VII by now.

The steady salvos from the next landing lit the stairwell. Chewbacca, checking it out with narrowed eyes,
gobbled something to Han.

"My pal's right," Han told the other defenders. "See
all the incoming bolts? They're hitting the far wall and
the other side of the floor, and that's all, nothing on
this side."

He slid around on the seat of his pants, cradling the
riot gun high across his chest. Chewbacca braced
Han's knees solidly to the floor. Han squirmed back
on his buttocks, centimeter by centimeter, until his
back was almost into the line of fire.

He and Chewbacca traded looks. The man's was
rueful, the Wookiee's concerned. "Hang it out."

Han let himself fall backward. The riot gun,
clamped across his chest, pointed straight upstairs. Still
dropping, he saw what he'd expected. A man in Espo
brown was stealing down the stairs, hugging the near
wall to avoid his covering fire. The scene burned into
Han's mind with an abrupt, almost painful clarity as
he cut loose with a flurry of shots. Without waiting to
see their effect, he leaned up again, long before his
back could touch the floor. Chewbacca felt the move,
pulled hard. Han came sliding to safety; his pop-up
appearance had begun and ended so suddenly that
nobody upstairs had managed to redirect his aim.

There was a rapid clattering on the stairs, and an
Espo-issue side arm spun to a stop on the landing. A
moment later, with a weighty bouncing, the pistol's
owner rolled to a halt next to it, more than adequately
dead. It was the Espo major.

Han nodded in tribute to the major's devotion to
duty.

The barrage from the next landing became more intense. The defenders answered with what weapons

they had. Chewbacca picked up a pistol dropped by one of the fallen defenders, a feathered creature lying in a pool of translucent blood. The corpse's beaked face had been partly obliterated by a blaster shot. The Wookiee found that the barrel of the pistol had been hit, and was twisted and useless.

Chewbacca, pointing at Han's empty, holstered blaster, threw him the unusable gun. Han threw back the riot gun in exchange and drew his own side arm, to charge it from the ruined pistol. Chewbacca, whose thick fingers didn't fit the human-sized weapon well, tore off the trigger guard, then began firing around the corner without looking—high, low, and in between, at every angle.

Han mated the adapters in the pistol's grip to those in his own blaster's power pack, just forward of the trigger guard. He wound up with only half-charge capacity, but it would have to do. Finished, he tossed the useless Espo pistol aside and joined the Wookiee. To frustrate counterfire, the two fired unpredictably, and they could be very unpredictable indeed. None of the Authority people seemed to want to emulate the major's heroism.

Suddenly the firing from above stopped. The defenders also stopped, watching for a trick. It occurred to Han that if Hirken had even one shock-grenade—but no; he'd have used it already.

A flat, hissing voice called down, "Solo! Viceprex Hirken would speak with you!"

Han leaned back against the wall nonchalantly. Without showing himself, he answered, "Send him down, Uul-Rha-Shan. What the hell, come on down yourself, old snake! Happy to oblige."

Then came Hirken's strong-sales-experience voice. "We'll talk from here, thanks. I know now just what it was you did."

Han wished to himself he'd known, too, beforehand. "I want to strike a bargain," Hirken went on. "However you're planning on getting away, I want you to take me with you. And the others with me, of course."

Of course. Han didn't even hesitate. "You got it.

Throw your guns down here and come down one at a time, hands on your—"

"Be serious, Solo!" Hirken interrupted, depriving Han of the chance to tell him where to put his hands. "We can keep you occupied here so that you won't be able to get out yourself! And Stars' End is at the top of its arc; we've seen that much through the dome. It'll be too late soon for any of us. What do you say to that?"

"No way, Hirken!" Han wasn't sure whether Hirken was bluffing about the tower's having reached apogee, but there was no way to check it short of leaning out one of the locks—a poor idea in view of the scarcity of spacesuits. "Hirken's dead center about one thing," he whispered. "They *could* pin us here if we let them make the rules."

The others followed him quickly down to the next landing, the last one before the tier-block level. They slipped around the corner and took up positions, waiting. Now it'd be the Viceprex's turn to sweat. From what Han could hear, it sounded like the majority of the prisoners were still in the tier blocks, unsure of what they should do. Han just hoped they wouldn't panic and come his way.

He had his blaster raised, knowing a questing head must come around the corner they'd abandoned, but it was impossible to anticipate exactly when it would come.

A head did flick around the corner, Uul-Rha-Shan's, high up; he'd stood on someone else's back or shoulders. He flashed out, saw the disposition of the defenders, and pulled back with astounding speed. Han's tardy shot merely chipped a little more wall away; the pilot marveled at how quickly the reptilian gunman had moved.

"Is that how it is to be, Solo," came Uul-Rha-Shan's hypnotic voice. "Must I hunt you from level to level? Strike a bargain with us; we only desire to live."

Han laughed. "Sure, it's just everybody *else* that you *don't* want to live."

There was a noise from below, boots on the stairs.

170

Doc reappeared, puffing. He threw himself down next to Han, his face composed in alarm. Han hand-signaled him to speak quietly so that those above wouldn't hear.

"Han, the Espos have come! Their assault craft is at the lower lock, unloading a strike force. They've linked up with the Authority people who were hiding from us down there. They drove us off the engineering levels; many were shot, and we were forced back. More died on the stairs before a rear guard was organized, but the Espos are pushing a heavy blaster up, step by step. We're in it where it's deep, this time!"

A stream of prisoners was already pouring frantically up the stairwell, bound for the only shelter left, the tier blocks. "The Espos down there have spacesuits on," Doc said. "What if they bleed off our air?"

Han abruptly saw that the men around him were looking to him for an answer, and thought, *Who, me? I'm just the getaway driver, remember?*

He shook his head. "I'm tapped out, Doc. Get yourself some machinery; we'll play them one last chorus."

Hirken's voice boomed down triumphantly. "Solo! My men just contacted me by com-link! Surrender now, or I'll leave you here!" As if to emphasize that, they heard the oscillation of a heavy blaster somewhere in Stars' End.

"Well, they'll still have to come through to us," Han muttered. He grabbed Doc's shirt, but recalling Hirken, spoke in a low, hard tone. "Don't sweat the air; the Espos can't bleed it off or they'll kill their Viceprex. That's why they hit the lower lock instead of the one at prisoner level; they knew they'd have a much better chance of getting in without having to burn and rupture the tower. Send up everyone you can, anyone who'll come. We'll rush Hirken, whatever it costs, and use him as a hostage."

Remembering the barrage the Authority people could lay down in the narrow stairwell, he knew that the price would be terrible. Doc did, too, and pushed himself off looking, for the first time, like the very tired old man he finally felt himself to be.

"Don't stop for anything," Han was telling the others. "If somebody falls, somebody else grabs his machinery, but *nobody stops.*"

He caught Chewbacca's eye. The Wookiee peeled back his lips from his curved fangs, scrunching his black nose, and sounded a savage, appalling howl, shaking his shaggy head—a Wookiee's way of defying death. Then he grinned and rumbled at Han, who smiled lopsidedly. They were close enough friends not to have to make any more of it than that.

XI

MORE inmates had come up to the landing, but they were unarmed. Han repeated instructions about weapons and not stopping. His heart pounded when he thought how concentrated the energy beams would be in that stairwell. Goodbye, Old Spacemen's Home.

He rose to a half crouch, and the others emulated him. "Chewie and me first, to lay down a cover. On three; one, two"—he edged to the corner—"th—"

A small, furry form, vaulting over those behind Han, landed on his shoulders, tugging at his neck. Its limber tail looped out to encircle the surprised Chewbacca's wrist.

Han staggered, valor forgotten. "What the flying—" He identified his assailant. *"Pakka!"*

The cub swung down from Han's neck, bouncing up and down urgently, tugging at his leg. For a moment no fact seemed reliable. "Pakka, didn't you, I mean, where's Atuarre? Dammit, kid, how'd you get here?" He remembered then that the cub couldn't answer.

Doc was shouting from below. "Solo, get down here!"

"Sit on things here; don't charge and don't fall back unless you have to," Han told Chewbacca. He pressed through his troops and raced down the stairs, trailing the fleet Pakka. Inside the emergency door leading to the tier blocks, he slid to a halt. *"Atuarre!"*

She was surrounded by Doc and the other prisoners. "Solo-Captain!" She seized his hands, her words tumbling out on top of one another. She'd brought in the *Millennium Falcon* and clamped onto the cargo lock here at the tier-block level, on the opposite side of the tower from the Espo assault ship.

"I don't think they noticed me; energy fluxes in Stars' End are distorting sensors completely. I had to link up purely by visual tracking."

Han drew Doc and Atuarre aside. "We could never, never fit all these people into the *Falcon,* not if we use every cubic centimeter of space. How do we tell them?"

The Trianii broke in. "Solo-Captain, *shut up!* Please. And listen: I have a tunnel-tube junction station secured to the *Falcon.* I drove it right up against the ship and made it fast with a tractor beam."

"We can certainly fit inmates in the tunnel-tubes if we extend them," Doc began.

Han's excited voice overbore him. "We'll do better than that. Atuarre, you're a genius! But will the tunnel-tube reach?"

"It should."

Doc was looking from one to the other. "What are you two— Oh! I *see!*" He rubbed his hands together, eyes bright. "This will be novel, for a fact."

One of the defenders from the upper landing poked his head through the emergency door. "Solo, the Viceprex is calling for you again."

"If I don't answer, he'll know something's doing. I'll send Chewie down to help you. Work fast!"

"Solo-Captain, we have only minutes remaining!"

He bounded up the stairs, though it left him huffing and heaving, and threatened to black him out. Air's going, he thought. In hushed tones he explained every-

173

thing quickly and dispatched the Wookiee and most of the others down to join Atuarre and Doc.

Then he answered Hirken. The Viceprex shouted, "Time's short, Solo. Will you yield?"

"Yield?" Han sputtered, unbelieving. "What d'you have in mind, defloration?" He pegged a shot around the corner, beginning a steady harassing fire, and hoped that those below could hold the Espo assault team for the required time.

Ninety seconds later a cycling light came on over one of the unused stern air locks of the Authority assault craft. No one was there to notice, because, except for a skeleton watch, the entire ship's complement had been turned out to rescue the Viceprex, at his order.

The lock opened. Through it stepped a very incensed Wookiee, hefting a captured wide-bore blaster. He was pleased, however, that he hadn't been compelled to waste time and power burning through the lock doors. He'd secured the outer hatch open. Behind him, floating in the weightlessness of the extended tunnel-tube, were more prisoners, waiting with weapons and with claws and stingers and pincers and bare, eager hands. Even farther back, at the junction station, other prisoners were being crowded aboard the *Falcon,* while more waited to leave the tower. Since the freighter could never hold them all, this ship had to be captured.

Chewbacca gave a hand motion and set off. The others drew themselves in after, touching down as they entered the assault craft's artificial gravity.

The lock's opening had been noted on the bridge. An Espo crewman, coming to check out what he thought would be a malfunction in the air-lock apparatus, rounded a corner and almost fetched up against the Wookiee's enormous, furry-haired torso. A stroke of the blaster's butt sent the Espo flying back through the air. He landed in a brown-clad heap, his helmet skittering along the deck.

Another Espo, down a side passageway, heard the

noise and came running, tugging at his holstered pistol. Chewbacca stepped out of concealment and swung the blaster's stovepipe barrel, downing him. As prisoners rushed to pick up the felled men's weapons, Chewbacca led the rest on, past engineering and crew's quarters, as small parties split off from the main group to take and hold those areas. More and more prisoners poured from the aft lock, making way quickly for the many who were to follow.

The Wookiee came to the hatch of the ship's bridge. He hit its release and, as the hatch slid up, stepped through. A junior officer did a foolish double take and fumbled for his pistol, saying, "How in—"

Chewbacca struck the officer down with a giant forearm, then threw his head back and roared. Those behind him surged into the bridge. Little of the fighting done in the next twelve seconds was with artificial weapons. None of the bridge watch ever reached an alarm button.

Setting the wide-bore aside, Chewbacca prepared to cast off from Stars' End.

Atuarre watched anxiously as she and a few chosen helpers in the big tier-level cargo lock almost threw milling prisoners into the tunnel-tube, where they thrashed like swimmers, moving and helping one another toward the junction station. Doc had already gone ahead to take the *Falcon*'s controls. As soon as Chewbacca had control of the assault craft, he was to free it gently from the tower so that it couldn't be retaken, and the Espos' withdrawal route would be cut off.

So many! Atuarre thought, hoping there'd be room enough for all of them. Then she saw a familiar face in the crowd and abandoned her place, keening with joy.

Pakka came, too, and clung to his father's back, holding on to both his parents for the first time in months, his wide eyes tearing.

Just then, Stars' End's general power conduits, weakened by erratic flow management, began to explode.

Up on the landing, Han heard it, the beginning of Stars' End's death throes. He was holding with three others, all of them armed. Hirken's people had been quiet for the last few minutes; the Viceprex was probably hoping that relief wasn't far off. And he could be right, since Espo assault troops were working their way up through the tower quickly, mowing down the prisoners' opposition.

But the exploding conduits constituted a new factor. Han ordered everybody back. "We'll hold at the tier-block level; pass the word below to come running." They could pull back to the air lock, which lay beyond the fifth tier block, if they had to.

He fired a few more shots up the stairwell as his runner took off. He tried to figure out how long it had been since the tower had been blown free. Twenty minutes? More? They were asking a great deal of their luck.

As Han and his men fell back, the clatter of the lower-level defenders was heard. Both groups met at the emergency door leading to the tier blocks and crowded through. Han, among the last, turned to give the man behind him a hand, only to see him die with an odd, disappointed look on his face.

Han pulled the falling body out of the way as the final prisoner leaped through. Several others helped him shoulder the ponderous door shut as blaster and disrupter fire lashed against it, and made it fast with scraps of metal jammed in the latch. But it wouldn't hold long, especially if the heavy crew-served blaster were brought up. Han surveyed the prisoners with him. "How many left to load?"

"Almost done, fella," someone called. "Just a few left, not more than a hundred or so."

"Then anybody who's not armed, hat up! The rest spread out and take up a firing position. We're almost home."

They were still moving down the corridor when the emergency door crumpled inward, burned from its frame in a rain of glowing slag. The snout of the crew-served blaster stood in the gap, pointing straight into the abandoned first-tier block. Han didn't bother firing at its shielded barrel.

The heavy blaster erupted into the empty tier block, and an armored Espo came worming around it to enter the corridor. One of the prisoners stopped long enough to shoot him. At the curve in the corridor, the defenders paused to take up firing again. The gunners were having trouble getting their piece through the emergency door without exposing themselves to counterfire.

Han and three others were the only ones left; a few prisoners had gone on to set up a new line of defense. Smoke from ruptured power conduits was getting thicker, the air thinner. Han's senses strayed for a moment. He was opposite the door to the second tier block and crossed to it, bent over double, for a better field of fire.

But he spied something propped up against one of the stasis booths, halfway down the tier's aisle. "Bollux, what the hell are you doing there?" Evidently the 'droid either had been dragged or had managed to drag himself this far toward the air lock, then had been shunted aside, and pausing in the shelter of the tier block for a moment, was unable to rise again. Han realized that no prisoner in fear of his life would have taken time to worry about an antiquated labor 'droid.

He ran to his side and dropped to one knee. "Up and at 'em, Annihilator. We're beatin' feet."

It took all his strength to get the 'droid up. "Thank you, Captain Solo," Bollux drawled. "Even with Max in direct linkage, I couldn't—*Captain!*"

Simultaneously with the 'droid's warning, Han felt Bollux throw all his mechanical weight against him, sending the two of them spinning around. In the same stopped frame, as it seemed, a disrupter beam meant for Han sliced into the 'droid's head.

As they spun, Han's draw was automatic. In that frozen instant, he saw Uul-Rha-Shan standing in the doorframe at the head of the aisle, the bodies of the other defenders on the corridor floor behind him.

The reptilian gunman had his weapon held at arm's length, knowing that his first shot had missed. The disrupter pistol was realigning. Han, with no time to aim, fired from the hip. Everything seemed to him to take forever, and yet to happen instantly.

The blaster bolt flowered high against Uul-Rha-Shan's green-scaled chest, lifting him and hurling him backward, while his own disrupter shot lanced upward and splashed off the ceiling.

Han and Bollux were sprawled together on the floor. There was no light in the 'droid's photoreceptors, no evidence of function. Han rose shakily, locked the fingers of his left hand around Bollux's shoulder pauldron, holding on to his blaster with his right, and began hauling, heaving for breath.

He never saw the Espos who, following in Uul-Rha-Shan's wake, were ready to cut him down. Nor did he see them fall, downed by the fire from the prisoners' counterattack. Han's lightheadedness had narrowed his vision down to a dark tunnel; through that tunnel he would drag Bollux back to the *Falcon,* nothing less.

Suddenly another figure was at his side, a furred and sinuous Trianii Ranger, bearing a smoking blaster. "Solo-Captain?" It was a male's voice. "Come, I will aid you. We have but seconds."

Han let the other do so, both of them tugging the 'droid's hulk along much more quickly. Dull curiosity made Han ask, "Why?"

"Because my mate, Atuarre, said not to bother coming back without you, and because my cub, Pakka, would have come if I had not." The Trianii called out, "Here, I've found him!"

Others arrived, to give supporting fire, throwing the Espos into a brief confusion. The assaulting troops, not having gotten their heavy blaster into the corridor yet, fell back. More willing hands dragged at Bollux.

Then, somehow, they were all standing at the air lock, and the Espos seemed to have broken off their attack. The 'droid was floated into the tunnel-tube, along with the other defenders and Atuarre's mate. Only then did Han enter the air lock, leaving behind a strangely silent chamber. The fresher, thicker air of the tube hit him like a drug. He waved the rest on.

The *Millennium Falcon* was still his ship, and he would be the one to cast off.

"Solo, wait!" A man stumbled out of the smoke. Viceprex Hirken, looking a century older. He spoke with hysterical speed.

"Solo, I know they've moved the assault ship away from the lower lock. I told no one, not even my wife. I ordered the Espos back and came in by myself."

He shuffled closer, hands imploring. Han stared at the Vice-President for Corporate Security as if he were a specimen under a scope.

"Please take me, Solo! Do anything-anything-anything to me, but don't leave me here to—"

Hirken's handsome face jumped, as if he'd forgotten what he was about to say, then he fell, squirming and reaching uselessly for the wound in his back. His obese wife came waddling up behind him with Espos at her back and a smoking pistol in her hands.

Han had already hit the inner air-lock hatch closure. He dived through the outer, into the tunnel-tube, hitting that switch, too. As the outer air-lock hatch closed, he irised the tunnel-tube shut, released its seal with an outgushing of air, and unclamped the tube. He floated there, watching through a viewport as Hirken's wife and the Espos beat at the air lock's outer-hatch viewport, unavailingly. Stars' End's descent speed had already drawn it away, and it plunged deeper into the planet's gravity well.

Around him he could see and hear the wobble of the tunnel-tube as packed prisoners were gradually absorbed into the assault craft and the *Millennium Falcon*.

Everyone in the two ships and the tunnel-tubes was so busy crowding elbow to pseudopod, or helping the injured or the dying, that only one survivor thought to watch the tower's fall.

As his mother and Doc labored over the *Falcon*'s controls, conning the freighter under its extreme burden and maintaining tractor-grip on the junction station, Pakka hung from an overhead conduit in the cockpit, the only one with both an unoccupied mind and a vantage point.

The cub stared down at Stars' End's descent, the flawless trajectory of an airless world. And even the sudden, brilliant flash of its impact didn't distract the others, who had lives to worry about. But Pakka, unblinking, unspeaking, saw the symbol of Authority flare and die with the brevity of a meteor.

The wind pulled hard across the landing field on Urdur, a no-nonsense wind, chilling, biting, but fresh and free. The former inmates of Stars' End, those who had lived to reach this latest outlaw-tech base, breathed it without complaint as they were herded off to temporary quarters.

But Han still pulled his borrowed greatcoat tighter around him. "I'm not arguing," he argued. "I just don't understand, is all." He was addressing Doc, but Jessa was listening, as were Pakka, Atuarre, and her mate, Keeheen.

Nearby rested the *Falcon,* the tunnel-tube junction still clamped to her side, and the Espo assault craft. Doc had guided both stuffy, overcrowded ships into quick contact with Jessa, and they'd been directed to this latest hide-out world.

Chewbacca was still onboard the *Falcon,* surveying the damage done to her since the last time he'd seen her. A new *yaup* of inconsolable sadness echoed from the ship each time he found another item of damage.

Doc, rather than reiterate his explanation, said, "Youngster, check the 'droid out for yourself. There." Outlaw-techs were just offloading Bollux's mutilated, beam-scorched form from the ship. An entire segment of his cranium had been shot away by Uul-Rha-Shan. At Doc's order, his men brought over the repulsor-lift handtruck with the 'droid strapped to it. With force bars and pinch-jacks, they prized open the plastron.

And there sat Blue Max, unscathed, running off his own power pack. Han leaned over him. "Uh, Maxie?"

The computer's voice still sounded like a child's.

"Captain Solo! Long time no see. In fact, long time no see anything."

"Gotcha. Sorry; things were really jumping this trip. Is Bollux in there with you for a fact?"

In response, he heard the unhurried drawl of the labor 'droid coming from Max's grille, sounding strangely high-pitched through the vocoder. "Right enough, Skipper. Blue Max was in direct link with me when the disrupter hit me. He pulled all my essential information and basic matrices down here, safe and sound with him, in microseconds. Imagine that? Naturally, I've lost a lot of specifics, but I guess I can always relearn camp sanitation procedures if I have to." The voice became dejected. "I suppose my body's unsalvageable, though."

"We'll get you a new one, Bollux," Doc promised. "One for both of you, a custom puff; you have my word. But now you have to go; my boys will make sure all that circuitry in there remains stable."

"Bollux," Han said, and found himself with nothing to say. He hit that problem from time to time. "Take it slow."

"I always do," the vocoder drawled.

"G'bye, Captain Solo!" Blue Max added.

Jessa, shading her eyes, pointed to the assault craft. "There's a problem we won't solve in the shop."

A dark-skinned figure sat by the ship's ramp, head bent to his chest. "He took his uncle's death pretty hard," Jessa continued. "Rekkon was quite a man; losing him would be hard on anybody." She looked to Han. Han was studiously looking elsewhere. He saw the boy's head come up from his private grief; he bore a startling resemblance to Rekkon.

"What do we do with him?" Jessa went on. "Most of the prisoners will find a new life somehow, even Torm's father and brother. The majority of them will leave the Corporate Sector; a few hotheads plan to take it to the courts, as if they had a prayer. But the boy's by far the youngest you rescued, and he's got no one now."

She was watching her father expectantly. Doc's eye-

brows shot up. "Don't goggle at me, girlie. I'm a cer-
tified businessman and criminal. I don't collect strays."

She giggled. "But you never turn them away, either.
And you always say there's always room for one more
at the table, we'll just—"

"—scramble the eggs," he anticipated her, "and wa-
ter the soup. I know. Well, I suppose I could at least
talk to the lad. He might have some usable aptitude,
hmm, yes. Atuarre, you worked with his uncle quite
closely; would you mind coming with me?"

Doc went off with all three Trianii at his side. Pakka
turned and flipped Han a parting wave, his other paw-
hand caught up in his father's.

Jessa looked at Han. "Well, Solo, thanks. See you
around." She turned to go.

He couldn't stifle an involuntary *"Hey!"* She turned
back with a cant to her head that let him know he'd
have to talk fast. Which he did. "I put my life—my
one and precious life, mind you—on the line for your
father—"

"—and all those other fine people," she cut in, "including your good friend Chewie—"

"—and went through a couple of types of hair-
raising situations, and all you have to say is *thanks?*"

She evinced shock. "Why, you only carried out your
part of our deal. And I carried out mine. What else
did you expect, a parade?"

He glared at her, hoping she'd wither from his gaze.
She didn't. He spun on his toe and headed for the *Fal-
con*'s ramp with long strides. "You win! Women, hah!
I've got the whole galaxy, sweetheart, the whole galaxy.
Who needs this?"

She caught up, whirled him around. Jessa looked
good even in cold-weather gear. "Numbskull! What's
wrong with striking another deal?"

His brow furrowed. I am somehow slipping into
something tricky here, he thought, but I can't quite
see what. "What kind of deal?"

She considered it, looking him over. "What are your
plans? Are you going to join this campaign against
the Authority? Or clear out of this part of space?"

He looked up, sighing. "You should know better than that. Rob 'em blind, that's my kind of revenge."

Jessa leaned around him and called up into the ship: "Hey, Chewie, how'd you like an all-new guidance system? And a complete overhaul?"

The Wookiee's delighted honks, preceding his appearance at the ramp, sounded like a happy foghorn. Jessa finished cheerily, "And to show you what a sport I am, boys, I'll throw in some body work, repair all minor hull damage. I'll reroute the ducting in the cockpit, too; get all those conduits and other head-knockers out of your way."

Chewbacca was close to tears of joy. He threw his hairy arm around the *Falcon*'s landing gear and gave it a wet Wookiee kiss.

Jessa said, "See, Solo? It's easy when you're the boss's daughter."

He was flummoxed. "Jess, what am I supposed to offer?"

She slipped her arm through his, grinning slyly. "What've you got, Han?" She led him away, ignoring his objections. His outbursts became fewer as the pair walked across the landing field toward the distant buildings. Halfway there, Chewbacca saw, Han held his greatcoat open so that she could slip into it, safe from the bitter winds of Urdur, though her own suit was quite well insulated.

Leaning casually on the *Falcon*, the Wookiee watched them go, and thought about what he and Han Solo could do with a ship milled and tuned fine by the full resources of the outlaw-techs. His muzzle wrinkled back from his fangs. He was glad for the breather they'd have here on Urdur.

But after that, everybody had best hang on to his cash with both hands.

ABOUT THE AUTHOR

BRIAN DALEY was born in rural New Jersey in 1947 and still resides there in a village most noteworthy as the home of Edgar Snow. After a four-year enlistment in the Army and holding down the usual odd jobs (waiter, bartender, loading-dock worker), Mr. Daley enrolled in college, where he began his first novel. *The Doomfarers of Coramonde* was published in 1977; its sequel, *The Starfollowers of Coramonde,* in 1979.

Exciting Space Adventure from DEL REY